TO ANN

NOVEMBER

ENJOY

BP Hull

GHOST FROM THE
HOLOCAUST

Barry P. Hall

authorHOUSE®

AuthorHouse™
1663 Liberty Drive
Bloomington, IN 47403
www.authorhouse.com
Phone: 1 (800) 839-8640

Published by AuthorHouse   09/29/2015

ISBN: 978-1-5049-5181-4 (sc)
ISBN: 978-1-5049-5182-1 (hc)
ISBN: 978-1-5049-5180-7 (e)

Library of Congress Control Number: 2015915652

Dedication Page

Thank you to my children: Darren, Melanie and Rebecca
who gave me the courage to complete this book.

Thank you to Neil Curran long time harness race driver and trainer

The leading horse suddenly reared into the air with more of a scream than a whinny. A second before it looked like a sure winner, now the driver in the sulky was holding on for dear life, the other horses quickly caught up and passed them on the way to the finish line. The horse still jumping and whinnying loudly bolted toward the infield. The driver fell off. The horse crashed into the infield fence and was hung up. He had broken his leg, it was dangling loosely from the stump. It would have to be put down. I hated that part of this business. Sundown Sheila, John's mare had won.

We went down to the winner's spot on the track to help John celebrate his win.

"What do you think it was that frightened that horse?" I asked John.

"I couldn't say. I didn't see anything unusual," said John. "That's the second one he's lost in a similar way in the past month. The other one broke stride like that in the middle of race and tried to jump the fence at the end of the turn. It was injured and had to be put down as well. That stable seems to be plagued this year."

"Who owns the horse?" asked George.

"A fellow by the name of Norm McKenzie. He has a horse farm out near Norwood. Toronto is where he mostly has his string," said John.

"The scream the horse let out made my hair stand on end. That's the first time I ever saw a horse do that without prompting. I had a book with an illustration once, it was called 'The Legend of Sleepy Hollow", it showed Ichabod Crane's horse rearing like that when confronted by the headless horseman," I said.

"There's no headless horseman around here but something certainly frightened it," said George.

Morrow Park Peterborough, was quite usual as a gathering place for the gang on a Friday or Saturday. I owned a couple of standardbred horses which John trained for me. George, Robert and myself could be found at the track on these occasions helping John cheer home his four footed charges. We didn't bet we just liked to watch them race. That being the last race we had an interest in we headed for the exit. With John's win it had been a successful afternoon. The horse that was put down had been a heavy favorite. John and Will, who was John's race driver as well as farm hand and assistant in every way, had bet on their horse and had gotten very good odds.

"Will you and Will be in for Sunday dinner at 2:00 PM as usual?" I asked John, as he led his horse away.

2

"Yes sir, best roast beef dinner going," said John. "We wouldn't miss it."

We were discussing the horse with the broken leg as we headed toward the car park." I hate to see a horse put down for whatever reason," I said, "but a broken leg can't be repaired.

"Turned my stomach completely," said a voice nearby, "I've never seen one with a broken leg before."

I turned to see a scruffy looking character standing beside Harry, the track manager.

"Not a very nice sight, I agree,' I replied, "and who are you sir?"

"Ralph's my name," he looked white and ill, grabbed his mouth and headed for the washrooms at a fast shamble.

"Who was that?" I asked Harry.

"Well his name is Ralph Davidge," said Harry. "He used to be called randy Ralph when he was younger, he was a devil with the ladies back in the early twenties. He met a real nice looking lady who knew how to handle him and got him away from that. He was a heavy drinker back then too, but she straightened him out. For the size of her she was a real holy terror. He has had a lot of troubles in his life. They married and had a son, who they doted on. They were quite successful and did well. Then the war came along, the son enlisted and was killed at Dunkirk. She got hit by a drunk driver shortly after that and died. He took it hard, and he is as you see him now. All the cops know him and watch out for him. He still goes around pinching girl's behinds and they have to take him to the drunk tank for the night. Let me introduce one of our security people to you fellows, this is Kurt Mueller."

We all replied, "Pleased to meet you Kurt." and shook hands.

"Don't worry about Ralph," said Harry, "we kind of keep an eye on him."

Sunday arrived with its usual quiet calm.

"Our church secretary was up to her normal self today, did you notice the bulletin?" asked George.

"What was it this time?" asked Robert.

"She wrote in the bulletin," 'Jim Oliver and Judy Smith were married on October 24 in the church. So ends a friendship that began in their school days.' "I truly don't know where she gets them all. She obviously doesn't proof read what she writes."

Our bizarre summer adventure had started, but we didn't realize it yet. It was a nice typical spring day, cool, but with the sun shining brightly. As usual we were gathered at my house, after church to enjoy one of Mrs. McGregor's roast beef dinners. John and Will had not turned up as his pride and joy, Sundown Sheila, had developed a case of colic.

Our group had started small but now we had seven regulars and a couple of guys that came once in a while.

My name is Ron Withers. I'm 56 years old. I'm five feet nine inches tall with a medium build, light brown hair now sprinkled liberally with gray and I was starting to add weight. I had been a school teacher before the war, born into an affluent family I didn't see the need to work any longer. The things I like to do best in this world need lots of free time. I am retired, so I have the time. I like to golf and fish as well as being lazy. I especially enjoy being lazy. Being lazy was okay, but all my life I never backed away from a challenge. 'Never give up' had always been my motto. I had been a pilot in the RCAF during the war and was shot down on a raid over Germany and had spent 6 months in a prison camp.

I am the possessor of a large house which is 35 years old now but built in a very prosperous era of Canadian history. It is situated in a better neighborhood of beautiful Peterborough in the province of Ontario. I own the house not because I need the large house, but because I like it. The house was built when there were servants living in the house, and for a large family, as well. My grandfather had built it, he liked ostentation, the bigger and gaudier the better was his motto.

"That was a fabulous dinner!" said Squadron Leader Robert Mackie, late of his Majesty's Air Force, fighter command,

Great Britain, as he relaxed in his chair. Robert didn't look like a prototypical British officer. He was over 6 feet tall with no mustache, lean and agile for all of his 60 plus years of age. After the war he had got his release and moved here to Peterborough for no particular reason but to get away. He had no one left from his family. They had been killed in an air raid on London, while he fought above. How he had ever been able to scrunch his six-foot frame into a fighter plane was a mystery, but he had done it long enough to earn Ace status. He wore, as usual, a white shirt, vest and tie with his gray trousers. Robert didn't smile very often.

"Mrs. MacGregor has a marvelous touch with a nice prime rib roast," said George. "How do you get her to cook on a Sunday?"

"I don't think she believes I can cook anything. She goes to the early Sunday service then rushes back here to cook our Sunday feast. She takes the Mondays as her day off, and advises me to eat leftovers. I like cold roast beef, so it works out. You don't get good cooks easily nowadays, so I treasure her," I said with satisfaction.

"How did you come to employ her in the first place?" persisted George.

"Well," I replied, "she was a Canadian war bride from Scotland. Her husband was shot down and killed on a bombing raid over Berlin. This was in the dying days of the war. He had some relatives here and she had no one left in Scotland so she came here afterward. Her relatives here are quite poor so she was looking for work and I heard she could cook. She's been with me since. She has the two young girls to look after, Patricia and Margaret, and she needed some income. Sandy MacGregor, her late husband, owned that small house, but not much else. Incidentally," I continued. "She has 'the sight'. She has predicted the craziest things sometimes and they always seem to happen as she says.

"Yes I've heard of people like that," said George.

George had been a detective inspector in the Toronto police force. He too had been in service to King and country for the duration of the war and had fought valiantly first in Italy then later in France. He was 65 years old, 5 foot 9 inches of lean muscle, intelligent and thoughtful, not given to quick decision. He loved to tell jokes and I loved a good joke, so this trait, I often thought, had tied us together from the start. Then to, we both like to be lazy.

"It's something buried deep in the Scottish gene pool, so they say," I said. "Well. Her first name is Morag. You can't get much more Scottish than that. She told me Saturday morning that she felt something was wrong. I guess it could have been the accident at the track or maybe John's mare coming down with colic this morning."

Our Sunday afternoon group had started off as just George and myself. We were both retired. We had both moved here to Peterborough in 1950 or about six years ago. George had been a friend of my father's. He was a chief of detectives for many years in Toronto. He was dressed as usual in his gray trousers with white shirt and tie. He had already taken off his tie. I had retired early from the every day work week, after first, my parents had passed away then shortly after my much loved wife. It didn't seem to make much sense to keep working. My grandfather had made a small fortune then passed most of it along to my father. My father had felt that the money should be working and had bought a lot of land as well as some good stocks. He had paid cash for the stock and thus didn't have to sell in the depression. The stocks had done well after the war. I was very comfortably set for life. My wife and I had two boys, who were doing well in their chosen walks of life. Robert we had met at the diner one day. Hence the start of what was now a Sunday tradition, our group of guys getting together to have a time of good fellowship.

Soon after we started our Sunday tradition John Smith, another of my father's acquaintances had started coming. He had a horse farm north of the city where he raised horses for harness racing. I have two horses in training and we discussed their training and racing together frequently. Unless some crisis was on at the farm he always cleaned up to come to church. John wasn't here today. He was worried about his best race horse.

Next to the group was Jim Martin, my banker, nearing retirement and divorced. We all went to the same church. Jim was dressed in a nice light suit, suitable for the weather we were having. He is slim and not at all athletic, but always good company. He enjoys the parlor games we usually play on these week-end get togethers. He just isn't a golfer. Golfing is one of our favorite pastimes.

Moishe was my tailor and had arrived here in Peterborough to set up shop after escaping Germany after the war. He had been a prisoner at Bergen-Belsen during the war as had Sam, his buddy. They had survived, just. They had a picture taken together when liberated. It was hard to imagine. They were nothing but skin and bones. They looked like skeletons or ghosts. You could easily count their ribs. They laughed about it now. Moishe was not over fat, but he was certainly not lean. Since he was a tailor he was always dapper. Today he was in a suit that was more suited to the south of Florida or the Caribbean. Moishe's friend had lately arrived. Sam, his friend was very well padded indeed. He was in Toronto today with his sister's family. Sam worked with Moishe in his tailor shop. They had a nice business going. We considered ourselves sort of a league of gentlemen.

"Where is John today?" Said Jim.

9

"His prize mare has come down with colic," replied Robert. "He was hoping to race her next Friday night but now I guess she'll have to be scratched. Too bad, she was in where she had a good chance of winning." We all liked to go and watch our horses race. Moishe and Sam were the exceptions. They viewed horses as being something to get them from place to place as they had in their youth. When they fell on hard times during the war, they had looked on horses as being quite tasty.

It had started out to be a nice day but had become windy and overcast as the afternoon wore on.

"Since we all seem to have finished our coffee, would anyone like something else," I asked, pretending to be the great host. Everyone declined as usual.

"How about a game of cards, or perhaps you would prefer billiards," I offered.

The options were discussed and a couple of games of whist was settled on as there were five of us. We repaired to the card room where I again offered something to lubricate the pipes while we played. "Mrs. MacGregor has gone home but left us a large pot of coffee, or we have tea or a punch that she prepared if you would prefer that," I said. Once everyone was settled with a cup of coffee or tea, we started with a game of whist.

"Moishe did you say Sam was in Toronto this weekend?" asked Jim

"Sam managed finally to get most of the family money out of Switzerland," Moishe said. "He went to Toronto to give his sister some. Her son is a gambler, and appears to be an unscrupulous character to say the least, and has been after Sam to give him some money. Sam doesn't like him, but he felt his sister should have a fair share. He was left the entire heritage when the parents died in the concentration camp. He was very blessed to survive himself. His sister, husband and family got out through Holland while they could. The rest of the family waited too long. The family was quite well off before the war. They had been smart enough to put their money in Switzerland."

"That was good of Sam," replied Jim

"Sam also realizes how easy it is to be cut off, so he made a will this week as well," said Moishe. "He left everything to his sister as he has no other relatives that he knows about. He doesn't like her son but family is family."

Robert who was persistent, somewhat like a British bull dog, had a habit of overbidding, so wound up losing. He was a good sport however and just laughed it off. It was now teeming down rain outside, we had several games of billiards while the

non-participants talked and watched the players. Here Robert
proved to have the best eye and steadiest hand.

"How many horses do you have in training with John out at the
farm?" asked Jim. He liked to keep abreast of his clients' affairs.

"I currently have two, but I do have my eye on a high ranked
claimer. A stallion only four years old. John mentioned he could
handle a couple of more inmates. He has that young Gransden boy
who is interested in race horses and wants a chance to work with
them."

"Can you afford another horse?" asked Robert with some
curiosity.

"Oh, don't worry about his money," George said. "He's got bags
of it."

"Well horses in training need a fair bit of money to sustain
them," observed Robert.

"I guess that's part of my problem with the tax men. One
problem being the sale of some of the useless property and the
expenses of owning race horses." I said. "My grandfather was very
successful. He was trained in geology in Edinburgh University in
Scotland. When he came here, he went north to look for gold. He
found a lot of it. He loved horse racing. However, even though he
bet on them, being Scots, it was never very much. He used to drag
me off to the races all the time when I was young. He just wanted

someone to go with. My father had a lot of the Scotsman in him and I think I do as well. However, I'm going to spend some of it on myself. I'll be leaving lots for my sons when the good Lord requires my soul," I added.

"In my opinion," remarked Robert. "If you have it, you should enjoy it."

The billiards had just ended, Jim looked at his watch and remarked. "It's just 10 minutes to eight, perhaps we can watch the "Ed Sullivan show" I believe they have something special on tonight."

"Oh that's just advertising. They have something special every Sunday," I replied. "I always try to watch, it's the best show on television. I think the head liner tonight is Jimmy Durante. He's a good comedian, but with that nose he looks like he's carrying a ski ramp around with him."

George rose and headed for the TV room. "I understand they have a way to send color pictures now. Have you heard about that?"

I moved after him. "Well I looked into it but very few programs are broadcast that way yet and the sets to receive color broadcasts cost a lot. When they have more programs on, I'll be looking into a set. Meanwhile we'll have to settle for black and white I guess. Did you know that television was developed in the 1920's but first began to be broadcast commercially in 1948?"

"The 1936 Olympic Games were carried on cable in Berlin and Leipzig," offered Moishe.

"I did not know that," I said.

At the moment George and I were the only ones in the group who had television sets. There were only two channels with sometimes three available. A station in Buffalo was sometimes available but quite snowy. I had the set about a year now, George less than 6 months. George watched the news every night, plus the "I Love Lucy" show. There was lots of other good shows but we never seemed to have the time to watch them.

Jim managed to get to his favorite seat. "I like "The George Burns and Gracie Allen" show. Good variety shows as well, like The Milton Berle show. The trouble is they take up so much time. There is hardly time to do anything else. I guess it's all right for shut ins and old folks."

I switched on the set and settled down with a glass of punch. "That new one "Gunsmoke" is one of my favorites but I don't get to watch it often. It's on late Saturday, so I usually don't stay up to that time." The opening of the show was just starting.

"Who would have thought a very few years ago that we would now be able to experience this quality of entertainment," said Jim. "I used to listen to "Gunsmoke" on the radio, with different actors. I never thought I'd see it in this manner. There are several old radio shows that have been converted to this new media but they don't seem as good somehow." The set had now warmed up and just in time. The opening theme song had just started. We settled back for what proved to be a very entertaining show.

As the closing credits were being run, Moishe got up saying. "I better go. There's a long work week ahead."

"Don't forget we are having a board game and jam session night, two weeks today, Sunday. Both you and Sam are invited as usual, and we're going to the track next Saturday to see my horse run," I said, following him to the door.

"I think Sam might go to your racing Saturday," replied Moishe, "but I have the accounting books to look after. It's the only chance I get."

"You work too hard." I reproved by way of a goodnight. With that Robert asked if we might have a game of cards. His game is bridge, but he quickly got out voted by the hometown crowd. Bowing gracefully to the inevitable, he said. "You always favor that unusual game you colonials play."

"What better way to wrap up the evening?" laughed Jim.

"We were all raised from very young to play Euchre," said George humorously.

"Yes I know," said Robert. "Next weekend perhaps I can talk you chaps into a decent game of Bridge."

The games, three in all proceeded in a lively manner. However everyone was tired by that time and the evening broke up.

The next week end being the May long week end, my sons and their families were due for a visit. At these times our Sunday afternoon get togethers were put on hold.

Chapter 2

Monday the week before my brood arrived, dawned bright and sunny so I decided to drive out and visit John. I wanted to inquire about his mare. Listening to the car radio on the way there I heard we were in for a nice sunny warm week. It was mid-May and we had not gotten our fishing tackle out yet. None of us was enough of a fanatic to go ice fishing, we liked warmth and comfort. We liked bass fishing best, but the bass season was still a couple of weeks away. Golfing was in full swing. Perhaps I could get some practice at the driving range this afternoon, and win one of the inevitable rounds later this week against George and Robert. I'm an early riser but when I arrived a couple of horses where already being exercised on the practice track. I recognized my gelding, Dorset Lightning which John was driving but not the other horse, his hired hand Will was driving that one. Will was a good worker. He liked horses and seemed to understand them well. He was illiterate but not stupid. He had grown up on a poor farm and wasn't sent to school often. His parents, now passed away, had been poor and needed him as help on their farm. Blessed with a slim build and a strong body, he seemed to have a telepathy toward horses and they responded well to him. He lived here on the farm, not in the main house, there was a small cottage on the property which John gave him to live in. He kept it neat. He had planted a nice vegetable garden out back from which he had fresh vegetables all summer. Just now peas and cucumbers were just getting usable. He had a green thumb, things seemed to grow well for him. He cooked and cleaned for himself and was generally a big plus around the farm. Will, who was about 45 years old, was dressed as usual in his overalls, he had other clothes but kept them strictly for visiting, which he did little of, or for church which he attended every week.

John had been left the farm by his parents when they passed away and it was all he knew. He was a trim 60 years old, tough as nails. His 6 foot frame carried a solid 165 pounds. He was always clean shaven, and kept himself tidy even though farming is not an occupation for someone who feels the need to be clean all the time. The farm was kept neat and tidy but generally was always in need of funds. They needed at least ten horses to make it viable but they usually struggled along with six or seven. I had helped him out a little here and there, but he was a very proud type and didn't like to take what he thought of as charity. John was older than I by a few years and had been very good friends with my parents, they had visited often to each other's houses. John's parents had known my grandfather as he was very into harness horse racing.

I parked beside the main barn, and John drove up almost immediately. John had never married and his cooking had never made him the least bit fat. He was dressed as usual in his overalls, which partially hid his plaid shirt. He as always had a smile on his face, it took a lot to get him in a bad humor or depressed. He handed the reins over to a young lad.

"This is Dave Gransden," John said, by way of introduction.

"I'm very pleased to meet you," I said

"Thank you sir. I'm pleased to meet you as well," replied Dave.

Dave was 19, I knew from what the rumor mill had passed along. He was dressed as Will and John in overalls and a shirt. He came from a big family that lived near Bobcaygeon and he wanted to be a horse trainer. John liked him, because, as he said, he was a good humored hard working type. He got along with the horses quite well, horses always seemed to know what the person was like. They liked people who treated them well. John also knew the family, as they were some kind of relatives, cousins I thought.

"Take him, cool him down and give him a nice bath," John said to Dave.

"How is your mare coming along?" I asked by way of greeting.

"The vet was here most of yesterday. She had a touch of colic but seems to be okay now," He replied hopping off the sulky.

"She'll be fine but I'm going to scratch her for Friday. She needs a bit more rest anyhow."

"We thought you might. We missed you for the Sunday evening festivities yesterday. Hope everything will be OK for two weeks yesterday. My sons are coming to visit next week-end. How's my old boy there for Friday?"

"Fairly bursting with energy. How are your sons and their families?"

"Every one of the family is healthy and the young ones are full of vim and vigour as usual. How do you think my horse will do against this crowd you have him in?"

"He won't disgrace himself. He should find most of the field as fairly easy competition, but there's an older gelding shipping in from Toronto that won big last week. Still, he has never done that well here before. They ship him in every few months or so. Always after a big win it seems. Maybe he doesn't like a half mile track or the water or something. He just never seems to be better than fifth or sixth here."

"That might be one of the oldest dodges in racing. My late grandfather as you know was a huge harness fan. He told me about a lot of things that are done by less than scrupulous racing stables. Have you still got all those old racing programs?"

"Sure they're in the house you can look at them all you want to, when we go in. What's on your mind?"

John had been around racing for a long while but was honest and rather unworldly, since he was honest he felt all other people were as well, "We'll look at the books on this horse first. I can't say for sure that they're doing anything even after we look at the statistics. How is business in general?"

"I've lined up a new owner. A fellow by the name of Jack Sheldrake. That's his gelding there with Will. He has two other horses for me that he's shipping in this week."

"I've met him and been told things about him as well. He moves his horses around a lot."

"Does he pay his bills? Is he dishonest in any way? Did you hear anything like that?"

"No. I must say I heard nothing like that about him. Just that he gets dissatisfied and moves."

"Well I don't want a deadbeat on my hands," said John.

"Oh I couldn't say that he's a problem that way, just that he's a tedious, impatient man."

"I think I'll reserve judgment but thanks for the advice. We can certainly use the business. Particularly as he has three to train." This would put the farm close to a money making proposition. I was very happy to hear that news, as I liked John and would like to see him successful. "I have other news for you. Do you remember that cheap claiming mare I got from that race two weeks ago? I have decided to breed her to Joe Handley's stallion. The stallion's bloodlines are good. In fact he won a couple of top notch races as a two and three year old. Joe charges a heavy price for stud service but he owes me a favor and has consented to give it back in that manner. The mare is no slouch herself having won a couple of top filly races before she got that virus and never recovered her speed. It's worth a try anyway."

"I never thought of you as raising a foal to race," I said. "I know you must have done it, but I only remember you having adult horses."

"Yes I've tried them a while ago, but for every ten you start with three or four will get to the races and maybe one will win a race. It's kind of expensive. This foal will have good bloodlines but will he be a racer is anybody's guess. Once in a while a miracle happens and a new colt can be a super star. We always live in hope. Both Will and I have some experience foaling and we just saw a course that's being given by a top stud farm on the subject. It's not too expensive and Will has said he'll go. It's being given down near London. The main object of the stable is to educate some stud grooms for themselves, but Will says he'd like to learn more. Anyway we applied for a spot and got in."

"You and Will astonish me. I didn't think you would be interested in things like that. I must say that once in a while I have thought about starting from scratch so to speak. I've never had a really well bred or top notch horse to start from. The thought of starting with an unknown has long intrigued me."

"Well hold that thought," said John, "My stables aren't big enough to hold all these horses. I too like the idea, but we can't put the cart before the horse, if you don't mind a bad pun. I need somewhere to stable them all over the winter months. I've been thinking of building an extra barn to hold more. I'll have to talk to Jim about a loan to do it though. It should go through, I paid off the last one I had on time and don't owe anything much, and I own the farm outright."

"That sounds good to me let me know what he says, he won't tell me, its bank business and not mine."

John headed toward the house said. "Now let's see if we can find those program books you're interested in. I may not have all the ones you want, as last year I couldn't keep up the subscriptions, as I was a bit short of money."

"We'll have to do the best we can then," I replied. When I got seated at the kitchen table John brought out several boxes filled with form books.

"Here we are," said John, dumping them on the table.

"I didn't realize how much there would be to it," I said totally amazed.

"It won't take as long as you think," said John, "We can work back from his last race. They run him about every couple of weeks. The program books have the horses racing that day listed on the back."

"Still, it's going to take a while. I guess we can each take a pile and dig out the ones he's racing in, then put them in date order."

"I'll put the coffee on," said John.

When he had the coffee on we started through the pile and quite soon we had a few recent ones showing Joe Boy's results. He had once been a top notch horse, but being a gelding he couldn't go to stud, so he had tumbled down the ranks of recent years. Still he appeared to race usually quite a bit below were you would think he could still compete.

After about half an hour we were joined by Dave and Will. They had cooled off the horses and let them out into one of the enclosures. It was time for their mid-morning break. Will went to the stove and began to prepare bacon, eggs and toast. Dave joined us, and soon we had a good size pile of books with Joe Boy in them. We took a break so that the farm people could eat their late breakfast. I got a refill on my coffee while arranging the books in date order as they ate.

"What are you doing with all those old program?" asked Will.

"Ron here thinks he may be able to tell us why Joe Boy wins at Toronto then loses when he gets here."

"He's old and doesn't have the energy for two races in a row," said Will.

"He is twelve," I replied. "While that's old for a race horse it's still only middle age. Horses like people don't always get feeble with middle age. Most athletes including humans start to taper off after middle age."

"My grandfather was a very strong man until he was well past seventy. I understand what you're getting at," said Will. "What do you think is the problem with Joe Boy?"

"I think they are using him to win big bets. They may be running him for several races without trying to win. Then when the odds have increased, they run him to win maybe at a lower class. Then they would clean up on the bets."

"The racing authorities would be looking for that. They would get fined or maybe get their license suspended," chimed in John.

"It would have to look like they were trying as hard as they could in the other losing races."

"That's not as hard to do as it looks sometimes," I said. "My grandfather told me if you give the horse a very hard work out the day of the race, that alone will tire it. They might also feed it with lots of salt and give it no water to drink, until just before the race then give it all it would drink. What would that do to the horse? He'd have a lot of water sloshing around in its stomach. It would weigh more as well, for a short period. Then to, they could take him back to Toronto from here and race him in a class that was too high for him for a race or two."

"That could do it all right," said Will thoughtfully. "Do you think that's what they are doing?"

"Well I can't say for certain, but the form certainly makes it look like it."

"Then they probably won't be trying too hard on Saturday," observed John, "Maybe we can get in some bets on a good thing."

"Since watching my grandfather, I don't ever bet on anything," I said, "You never know what the other barn is thinking and what they will do. I've got to run anyhow or I'll be late for my lunch and golf date with Robert and George. Got to keep fit you know."

"Well we don't mind betting," said Will. "We never bet much, but for something like this we might put $10.00 or 20.00 dollars on our horse to win it. I know in lots of ways that's a lot of money, but an opportunity like this doesn't come along very often. I think you have the horse to maybe beat him anyway, you've got a good one there. He's just hitting his stride. You'll see."

Robert and George had just arrived as I drew up to the golf club house for lunch. As we walked in I told them the news from the farm. The lunch was always good at the Club. None of us felt like going home to scrounge up something to eat. We golfed most days when we were around, but we all liked fishing best. The peace and quiet appealed to all three of us. Bass season wasn't in just yet but we could stay in the deep water to avoid the nests and fish for pickerel and muskies. Pan fish were good eating as well, if we couldn't get the bigger game fish. There was always trout fishing, with several good streams near my cottage. We just didn't know where to go for them.

George was agitated and when we sat down he said, "Did you hear about the robbery which happened yesterday? An elderly neighbor of mine. She came home Sunday after going out to get a loaf of bread and surprised the thief. He hit her two or three times hard, then nearly choked her to death. When she passed out he took all her valuables that he had gathered up and fled. He must have gone out the back way. Our neighbor across the street saw her crawl out the front door when she came around and she called the police. She's in hospital in pretty rough shape. Apparently this is the third time this guy has struck. He sounds like he's pretty violent. Smashes up a lot of things and throws stuff around, very childlike. The police have been thinking it was teenagers, but she

did tell her neighbor it was a man, before she passed out again.
Still, that's not unusual in that type of thief. If he keeps getting
away with it he might kill someday. I've known it to progress
that way."

"Did he steal much?" asked Robert.

"Not much, but all her silver is gone, and she did have quite
a collection. It's not known yet what else, as she was taken off
to hospital and no one knows what else she had. I'd like to get
him aside for a little while. She's a nice old lady and this will be
devastating for her. The other times have been at night. They think
he watches places and finds out when the owners will be away then
goes in when he has lots of time. Maybe he thought she had gone to
church and would be away for a while. Generally he has taken TVs,
radios and things of that nature. He did take a silver service before.
The police haven't even got a description of him as this is the first
time someone has actually seen him."

"Has she not told them what he looks like," said Robert.

"She's been put to sleep to help her heal. She's pretty frail.
They're not sure yet if she'll pull through."

We finished eating our lunch by discussing the robberies. There
was nothing more we could add. The perpetrator seemed like a real
violent creep. It seems he made a habit of preying on older more

helpless people, but at least one of his victims had been a young family.

Our tee time was fast approaching so we grabbed our clubs and headed for a few practice putts before teeing off. All three of us enjoyed the game, but we never got very serious about it. We each shot our normal round. Robert shot 97. I had done better than usual but not anything to write home about, a 95. George had finished with 102. No improvement from last time out. None of us would ever turn pro, that was for sure. It had been a great day. We were now all tired and ready to head home.

"We should hit the practice range and drive a bucket or two of balls," remarked Robert.

"We always say that, but we never get there," I replied.

"Let's make a date for Thursday morning 9 A.M. and be done with it," said Robert. "I'll see if we need an appointment, and we'll all go regardless."

"OK by me," I said.

"Me too," said George.

Robert always said that every Monday, but we had been at it for many years and it was a well-established habit. Still he appeared to be more adamant than usual about some practice.

"I'm tired of getting nowhere with my golf game. I really do want to get better, I hope you two feel the same, because this time I'm really going to set something up," He said in a distinctly determined fashion.

"Everybody up for coffee and talk tomorrow morning," I asked.

"Yes sir, usual place and time I assume," said Robert. He got a course of nods as reply.

I headed for the driving range as I had promised myself, all the while thinking to myself, 'maybe I can get one up on those guys.' I drove a small bucket of balls as a starting amount. My driving actually seemed to improve toward the end of the bucket. The biggest problem however was short chips to the green. This session at least gave me the idea to try that with the next bucket.

Chapter 3

Next morning, we all arrived at the diner almost at the same time. As the weatherman had predicted it was a beautiful spring day, hardly a cloud in the sky, birds of all sorts making a tuneful racket. Most of them had a new family on the go. The diner was crowded as usual. Many people for their breakfasts as well as people just getting a coffee to take to work. George was clearly upset, he wouldn't tell us why until we were served. George and Robert ordered bacon, eggs, toast and coffee. Just coffee and toast for me. It being Mrs. MacGregor's day off. She would have a busy week of it. My clan would arrive Friday night, she would make up six bedrooms for them. She kept the rooms clean, but the beds were unmade. I only used one of the bathrooms, but they always expected all to be clean and of use.

"What news of the robbery," I asked George, after we had been served.

"My neighbor across the road, Mrs. Wilson, the lady that called in the emergency, is going to see her today. Apparently she's feeling better. Mrs. Wilson is going to see if she can do a little cleaning for her. If she gets permission I've volunteered to help her. She is quite a capable person, but apparently the place is a mess.

Mrs. Wilson's husband was killed in the war. She doesn't have much, but she keeps cheerful and works hard keeping her place neat. She knows Mrs. Johnson, the victim quite well."

"Why don't we all go to make the work go faster, you said the thief had made a real mess," volunteered Robert. "We have nothing better to do, except golf and this would give us a nice change."

"Making a mess is one of the things he always does apparently," replied George. "I guess we could all help. Mrs. Wilson should be back from her visit to the hospital about ten this morning. We can drive around then and see how she made out."

The waitress brought over the coffee pot for refills. "Would you guys like anything else?" she inquired. We accepted more coffee with thanks and declined anything else.

"I went around to the driving range after golf last evening," said Robert. "No appointment necessary during the week, as long as it's before five in the afternoon. It gets busy sometimes after that. I told him we'd be there Thursday at nine in the morning. So, now we have to go or you'll embarrass me."

We lingered over a third coffee, then as it was getting close to when Mrs. Wilson should be getting back from seeing her neighbor, Mrs. Johnson at the hospital, we headed for George's place. Since Mrs. Wilson had not yet returned from her visit to the hospital, we sat on George's veranda and discussed the cruelty and unfeelingness of people like this thief.

"If a person is desperate they will do many desperate things," pointed out Robert. "Of course we don't know if this guy is desperate or just malicious."

"That's quite true," I said. "We shouldn't judge at any time, not even in circumstance like this."

"It does make a person angry though, when they do cruel, malicious things to gratify their own sense of what's right."

We went to George's house to wait. It wasn't long before Mrs. Wilson came walking up the street on her return from the hospital. She was a small person, about 50 years old wearing a long print dress that was no doubt her good dress, but had seen better days. We went out to meet her and inquire how Mrs. Johnson was feeling.

"She's much better," said Mrs. Wilson. "And she has given me permission to straighten out the house. She didn't want to at first as she feels the house is old and run down and was embarrassed. I convinced her it didn't matter and mentioned that it would be much nicer for her to return to a clean house."

"We've all come to help," I said. "Provided it is okay with both her and you.

"Let's go and look at the damage," she replied. "I haven't been in there since it happened, but the police say it's a real mess."

She produced the key and we went to the front door. The screen door needed new screen and the front main door was badly in need of paint.

"I can see what she means," said Robert. "I guess she has neither the money nor the energy to fix these things up."

We entered the main part of the house, the corridor was okay, but on entering the kitchen the mess was truly appalling. There was sugar and flour among other things strewn all over everything mixed with a few eggs and the milk from the fridge. Other foodstuff as well as all the canned goods from the shelves. Dishes of all sorts were all over, some broken others still whole only by chance. On top of that the powder used by the police for collecting fingerprints was on everything as well. The living room and dining room were also in bad shape with furniture knocked over and fingerprint dust all over in here as well.

"Oh dear," said Mrs. Wilson. "She doesn't have a vacuum cleaner and neither do I."

"I have one," I said. "I'll go and get it while you start general tidying."

We might as well do a few other things for her while we're at it," said George. "I've got some paint left over from a project last year which is about the same color as the front door. I believe I might even have some screening to fix the screen door. I'll just go home and see what I can find."

When I returned George was busy fixing some new screening in the screen door. He had obviously found some. "I think I have enough of this paint to do those two Muskoka chairs she has here on the veranda, as well," he said.

When I got inside with the vacuum, Mrs. Wilson grabbed it and immediately started on the living room. The furniture had been turned upright and I could hear Robert in the kitchen, working to straighten up in there. I left Mrs. Wilson to it and went into the kitchen to help Robert.

"I can handle this," he said, "why don't you see what the upstairs is like. We haven't been up there as yet."

"Let's hope it's not like down here," I replied and headed for the staircase.

There was only one bedroom that was obviously used and things were strewn around, but not too badly. Some clothes however had been ripped. Again fingerprint dust was on everything. First I picked up the clothes and put them back on hangers. Keeping the torn ones separate, Mrs. Johnson may wish to repair them. She was a very poor lady, with only the small old age pension to rely on. Having straightened the furniture as well as

I could, I went in search of Mrs. Wilson to see if she had any dust cloths. She was finished vacuuming and dusting the living room and was headed for the kitchen. She said she had gone to her house to get some rags for dusting as she hadn't found anything suitable here.

"We've got a good start going here, but maybe it's time for a spot of lunch. I'll go and get some scones, a jar of jam, some cheese and whatever else I can think of. Perhaps you could make us some tea or coffee. We can stop when I get back and have something to eat. I noticed on the way down stairs, the carpeting on the stairs is in bad need of repair. I have a nice strip of stuff in my basement and some of those rods to hold it down. I'll bring those back at the same time."

"I hope she won't take offense," said Mrs. Wilson." Old people can be very proud that way, although in most ways she's a humble soul. I'll make some tea."

"We'll tell her what's done is done and beg her forgiveness for having taken the liberty."

On my return all work had stopped when Robert had started to clean up the major flour pile, he had found a man's pocket knife buried under the mess. George had promptly gone to his house next door and called the police. Mrs. Johnson did not have a phone. We sat down and had our lunch while waiting for the police. George

had found the back door in much the same condition as the front
and was going to start on that after lunch. Robert and Mrs. Wilson
where going to finish the kitchen, so I was elected to do the stairs.
Robert had found the small fridge was not working and tracked
it down to a fuse. George had gone next door and got one of his
spares. Power was restored and things were put in the fridge,
nothing much had been in it before, just some milk and a few
eggs. The milk was all over the floor with the flour and such. Mrs.
Johnson must have come back before he smashed everything. The
police came and without saying much had removed the knife. We
resumed work and had everything finished by early afternoon, so
we took Mrs. Wilson to an early dinner. We felt we had done some
good work. The restaurant was just our local diner but served good
home style meals. We had a good time.

Next morning for something different I strolled down to the
barber shop at the end of the street. I had just come to listen to the
gossip. The barber chair was empty so I told him to give me a trim.
The main topic of conversation was the robbery at Mrs. Johnson's.
They all wanted to know if I knew more than they did. I had to
disappoint them, but told them we had got her permission to clean
up and had done so the previous day. They were astounded at the
amount of mess the robber had caused. Some of the men were
well up in years and worried about themselves. They resolved to

lock their doors more often. I thought but didn't say that locked doors only resulted in broken locks or windows if the burglary was determined. I spent some of the afternoon on a short nap, then I headed for the driving range for some personal practice on chip shots.

For supper Mrs. MacGregor had made a nice beef stew, with apple pie for dessert. It was a good thing I liked apple pie. She had laid out some cheese and there was ice cream to go with it. How was I ever going to lose some weight with this kind of meal staring at me?

Thursday found Robert, George, and I at the driving range finally. We each got a large bucket of driving range balls and headed for the practice tees.

George said. "My son on the police force here told me the pocket knife we found in Mrs. Johnson's kitchen, was her own late husband's. I guess we had all hoped to help in the investigation, but it was a nothing clue."

"Well you can't win them all," I replied. "Now let's see what we can do with these practice balls."

We started off hitting balls one after the other with little concentration, more as a chore. The result was that every second ball flew in entirely the wrong direction. Duck hooks, slices, topped balls everything one could imagine.

"Perhaps we should try harder to concentrate and see if we can't do better than this," suggested George. "I've hit everything but a nice long straight drive."

We all agreed, the wildness is what did all of us in every time, and was the main reason we had trouble breaking 100. We began to take it slower and more serious. The results kept improving until we got to the bottom of our buckets.

"You know," observed Robert. "Now is probably the time we should head to the club and shoot a round. It's still early why don't we go to the club, have some lunch and see if we can get a tee time for after lunch."

"Alright by me. I've never tried golfing after such a practice as we just had. Usually after just a few practice putts," I replied.

We followed the plan and were pleasantly surprised Robert and George both shot under 93. I wound up with 102. Oh well I thought, this isn't as easy as it first appeared.

Friday was usually a day for us to go and watch a horse or two of John's race, he had nothing, but my horse on Saturday, the result of his mare's colic. We spent our day bumming around town. We could have gone fishing on Little lake or the Otonabee River but as it bass season had not arrived we felt that it was too soon. First we went to the cafe. Then a visit to Moishe and Sam at the tailor shop that Moishe owned. We were gathered on George's porch when his neighbor Mrs. Wilson came over, to tell us that Mrs. Johnson was feeling much better, and getting restless at the hospital. She wanted to come home. She knew she would feel apprehensive about being there alone, but Mrs. Wilson said she would keep an eye on the house and watch over her. She also felt she would feel less depressed at home. She would be discharged later that afternoon and Mrs. Wilson asked if we could go and bring her home. There was no bus that came near and taxis were very expensive. I gladly volunteered to get her. Mrs. Wilson was getting a casserole together and would eat supper with her. I drove over to the hospital and picked her up. She thanked me so often I felt embarrassed that I hadn't thought of it myself. When she saw how we had cleaned up and fixed a few things, she completely broke down. She was profuse in her thanks to us and begged us to forgive her as she felt there was no way she could repay us. We all explained, quite embarrassed, that we wanted no payment, besides it was just spare things laying around our place, going to rust, we just felt she'd been through enough.

"I knew you were Christians but I never expected this," she exclaimed. "When I was a young girl and into my teens, we always went to church, but my husband never believed in that, so we never went. I wish I had insisted. I sort of miss those days. My friend at the retirement residence went every Sunday, and used to ask me, but I never went and now it's too late to go with her."

"I could take you on Sunday, Mrs. Wilson as well if you wish, my car is certainly big enough," offered George. "I'll be getting there a little sooner than most, because I usually usher, but I could introduce you to the pastor and his wife, and they could get you settled. Make you feel welcome and that sort of thing."

"I would love that," said Mrs. Johnson, and was echoed by Mrs. Wilson.

"It's all set then," said George. "Be ready about 10:15 AM Sunday, the service starts at 11:00."

In due course, on Friday, the boys and their families arrived for the week end. We had a terrific time together, possibly the best in recent years. We did the inevitable trip to the lift lock to watch the boats being locked through. We also drove out to Little lake and had a nice walk. The usual games of cards and board games took up the evening, with the young ones watching television and playing some games as well. This type of thing happened every two months or thereabouts, and always wore me out. They were both good sons but had their own families to keep them busy. James, the oldest was married to June. They had two daughters, Vivian and Lilah. Malcolm, the younger brother, was married to

Sandra, they had a boy and a girl, who were called Aussie and Brook. James had a busy legal career as a junior in a large Toronto office. Malcolm was an accountant and worked on his own, out of his house.

With all the properties my father had bought I had given Malcolm and Sandra the use and upkeep of the large cottage property on Lake Rosseau as well as a house in Toronto. They spent most of their summer at the lake. James and June had the property on Indian Point on Balsam Lake near Coboconk, as well as another of the city properties, and spent most of their summer there. The big house where I lived in Peterborough had been built by my Grandfather. He liked things big and pretentious. Maybe I did as well. He had many servants in his day and the house had many bedrooms as well as other rooms that were in this day and age completely unneeded. It was however large enough so that all of my clan had a room for themselves when they came to see me. The house always sounded like an echo chamber when they had departed Sunday night. That was fine by me.

The following day we were all anxious to see what my gelding could do against the big runner from Toronto. We lined up Mrs. Wilson to look after the children when we went to the track for the day. Mrs. Johnson came over to keep her company. Mrs. MacGregor was extremely agitated all day. She kept saying she could see this black cloud. She said it was evil somewhere about. We invited Moishe and Sam. Moishe begged off as always as he did the books after the store closed on Saturday. Sam decided to come. He wanted to see what all the excitement was about. We arrived early and I went to seek out John and Will to see how my horse had shipped from the farm. Walking in from the car park, I met Sam and Jim from our crowd. They had both decided to come. Ralph met us, obviously drunk, and advised us not to bet on Rover Boy in the fifth, he told us the stable were going to stiff the horse.

"Don't bother the gentlemen, Ralph," said Kurt, who was standing nearby.

"That's quite all right," I told Kurt. "Thank you, Ralph, We appreciate your help. It's nice to see you again. How would you like to come to my place for Sunday afternoon dinner? No need to dress up. It'll be a good roast beef dinner with all the trimmings. I could pick you up around 12:00 or 12:30."

"I can always do with a square meal," he said. "I do remember you from the other night, but we hardly know each other."

He didn't appear as drunk as he had first come across I thought, "Well, all the better to get to know each other. Let me write down your address, I'll pick you up Sunday."

"Why invite him?" said Robert.

"He just seems kind of lonely and could do with a few friends. If he turns out to be a problem, we can always deal with that later. Let's wait and see." We had got to the stables by this time.

"I can see you're anxious," said John. "He's in good shape. Fairly bursting from his skin. He should have little problem with this bunch. Providing of course that what we think is true about the Toronto horse. He's here and looks fit."

"I don't know," I said, "this is the highest class he has run in."

"Don't fret, he'll not disgrace himself," soothed John. "Dave here is going to put a bet on him and so are Will and myself. We're quite confident in his chances. You don't bet I know but this is the best chance I've seen in a while."

"Just don't bet the farm, and Dave, I hope you don't think you can get rich this way. It never happens, no matter how skilled the person picking winners. You know Jim," I continued, changing the subject. "There is no such horse as Rover Boy anywhere on the program. Where did that Davidge fellow get that information from?"

"Oh, he rarely gets his facts straight anymore," said Jim.

Time seemed to fly by and our race was soon next up. "I can see what the attraction is, but it's too uncertain as to outcome, for me to bet anything," commented Sam. "However watching has its fascination. Of course it must be better if one has a horse of one's own."

"That's the attraction for me. It's like having a son who is doing well. You want to be there in his moment of triumph, or to console him in defeat. Triumph is much better, it gives you a good feeling," I replied.

The starter called the horses, which lined up behind the gate. The race was starting. The gates banged open and Joe's Boy, the Toronto horse quickly took the lead and set the pace. Our horse, Dorset Lightening quietly laying fourth. As the field of horses came by the grandstand the first time, the third place horse pulled out in a short burst to try to pass the leader. "Too soon." murmured George. When they turned into the back straight the horse that had been third started to fall back and it looked as if our horse would be boxed in. But the third place horse faded fast and we were able to get out as we started into the final turn. Our driver, Will started urging him quickly and sure enough Joe's Boy began to fade. His driver too was urging him but he appeared to have nothing left. We swept by to finish first easily while the horse who had been second all along was able to hang on for second. Joe's Boy finished fifth. We all trouped down to get our picture taken with the winner.

"I never get tired of the feeling I get when my horse wins," I commented to the group at large.

Dave and Will were in seventh heaven. They had each won a

month's pay. John had won even more. For me, the purse Dorset Lightening had won would pay the stabling cost for two months.

When the excitement had died down, Sam said it wasn't his thing and he was going to have a look around then head for home.

"Don't forget next Sunday's dinner and games at my house," I reminded. "We're having a board's game night."

"I'll be there I look forward to our Sunday gatherings," replied Sam.

After the race I went with John and company to see how my horse looked as he settled down. We had just reached our stall when there was a shattering scream, very high pitched and imperative. It turned out to be a horse, and he must be very stressed as he kept it up. There was several crashes then a horse raced down the aisle, running hard. Everyone was yelling. The horse crashed into the end of the barn. Since he could go no further that way he spun on his heels and came roaring back up the aisle past us again. We kept out of the way as well as we could. Whatever was bothering the horse was obviously extreme to the horse. Several people tried to stop him or catch him, with no success. He kept crashing into stalls, he was bleeding profusely. Finally one of the security guards pulled his pistol and shot him in the head from close range. The horse went down and lay there on his side quivering. He was dead.

Chapter 4

George and I arrived at church almost at the same time. He had the two ladies with him and introduced them to the Pastor and his wife, who made a fuss over them, helped to find them a seat and programs for the service. George and I went to pick up supplies to greet people with, and usher them in. The service went well. The secretary that typed up the bulletin had made one of her usual blunders.

She had typed "Ladies, don't forget the rummage sale. It's a chance to get rid of those things not worth keeping around the house. Bring your husbands." amusing as usual.

On the way out our friends Mrs. Wilson and Johnson were all aglow. They'd had a good time. I invited them home to share our roast beef dinner. I had to assure them that there was plenty for all. I told them I had also invited Mr. Davidge. They didn't know him, but I filled them in on a little of his background. I told them I thought he maybe needed a friend or two who could maybe get him off the booze and help him to turn things around. Mrs. Wilson and Ralph hit it off right away. It seemed as if he hadn't lost his appeal for the ladies. They insisted on serving. Including my gang we had thirteen for lunch. A bad omen Mrs.

Macgregor would have said. After the delicious main course the ladies brought out two strawberry/rhubarb pies. When I told them there was some whipping cream in the fridge, they went and made it up. With or without the whipping cream, the pie was delicious. Mrs. MacGregor certainly knew how to make pastry. Both ladies insisted that the meal was the best they'd had in a long while. We sat on the veranda for a while some in comfort, some who had eaten too much, uncomfortable. The ladies then said they would do the dishes. I said there was no need. However they said that the dishes couldn't be left dirty. Never argue with a lady, had been one of my father's favorite sayings. My two daughters-in-law loudly agreed with them. The four of them headed for the kitchen. We men relaxed until they finished. When asked if they wished to stay for games, they said it would be a nice way to cap the day.

The four ladies opted for Parcheesi. The rest of us got out the Monopoly board. The children for television. Three games of Parcheesi later, two having been won by Mrs. Wilson, they said they were tired, it having been a most exciting day. I drove them and Ralph home. My son Malcolm had easily won the Monopoly game. He had an exceedingly good grasp of business.

Once again Monday found me heading to the farm. I wanted to see how Dorset Lightening had come out of the race. John was on the practice track with him and Will each exercising a horse. I

recognized neither horse. John finished jogging his horse and drove
into the yard. Dave came out to get the horse to cool her, unhitch
her and turn her out. "Is that one of Jack Sheldrake's horses," I
asked John.

"Yes," he said "a good little mare quite willing and with a good
mouth. She has potential."

"How did Dorset Lightening come out of the race?"

"Good as gold. He ate up his meal after the race. I think he's
fit enough for next week end as well. I'd like to try him up a class.
There's a good race for him Friday, if that's okay by you."

"Sounds good to me. How is my mare Betty's Dream doing?"

"She seems to have developed a good case of the slows. I guess
I could try her in the lowest class on Friday, so you would have
two runners. I wouldn't count on her chances though. She has such
good breeding, it's a shame she isn't faster,"

"Well we can decide on her future after that. There's no hurry.
I did want to ask you what your thoughts are about me claiming
Kingston Kenny. I've been following him. He's in a high class
claimer here Friday."

"He's a good strong young horse," said John thoughtfully. "He
did lose last time out to that decent mare from Toronto. I thought
he would have beaten her."

"I saw the race myself, he looked to me to be in an amorous mood. Maybe she was coming into heat. If so he certainly wouldn't pass her. More like run along side trying to say 'look at me, look at me.'"

"Yes that could be it. Sometimes only horses know. That's a lot of money to pay for a horse, even if it is a claimer. It won a few races at two and three years old, and against some top notch horses. It wasn't classed among the very top though. Well it's your money," said John. "You could do worse. I can make out the forms and we'll submit them. Then we'll have to wait and see."

I dropped into the barn where Dorset Lightening was at present. He looked good to me. Glossy coat, the picture of good health. John fed and generally looked after the horses in his care, very well.

Robert hadn't arrived when I got to the golf course. George was there and as we greeted each other, the manager came rushing up.

"You've just had a call from your friend Moishe, he's at the police station, something dreadful has happened," he said. "He asked if you were here could you come down there."

George and I jumped in my car and got to the police station as quickly as possible. Moishe, as we could immediately see was in a terrible state.

"It's Sam," exclaimed Moishe. "He's been murdered by that thief. He didn't come in to work this morning so I went to his house, to see if he was sick. The door was unlocked so I went in. I have seen some truly horrible things in my life but this was the worst. The thief had taped his mouth and nose shut and so he suffocated to death!"

"How do you know it was the thief," asked George, visibly upset.

"His things were thrown all over, just as you described from the previous thefts. His new television is gone as well as his wallet and I don't know what else."

"That doesn't mean it was the thief," said George. "It certainly sounds like the thief, but it could have been anybody. Did he have any enemies? Anybody he owed money, or anything like that."

We respected George's knowledge in these matters.

No, no nothing, "replied Moishe.

"Here sit down Moishe," I said leading him to a bench set against the wall.

"You've had a terrible shock and you're not thinking clearly. How long have you been here? Can we get you a drink of something? We must be calm and think clearly for Sam's sake. Do they have a lunch room here perhaps we could get you a cup of tea?"

There was nowhere in the police station to get coffee or tea. We talked to the policeman in charge and were told we could leave.

They did take our names and addresses so that they could contact us later if needed. George's house was closest so we went there.

"Sorry I don't have anything stronger than coffee," George said as he led us in. He hurried to the kitchen to make it while we seated ourselves in his living room. When we were seated Moishe started to talk, but I persuaded him to compose himself and wait until we were drinking the coffee.

We were seated drinking coffee and eating some cookies when George said to Moishe. "Now maybe you can start at the beginning. Go slowly and mention everything you can think of that you saw or heard the police saying. Take your time and think hard. Start right from the time you left the shop," George was an old hand at this sort of thing. He'd seen all sorts of violent crime in his days on the force.

Moishe took a big gulp of coffee to wash down the cookie he was eating and began. "I left the shop before noon and went to Sam's place. I thought maybe he was sick or something. He didn't have a phone so I couldn't call him. When I got there I knocked but there was no answer. I tried the door and it was unlocked. I went in and the first thing I noticed was things flung all over, flour, sugar, coffee a terrible mess. Sam was not the greatest house keeper, but better than that. His living room is also the dining room and this was a terrible mess. That's when I went into the bedroom. He was on the bed. It was terrible. I still can't believe it."

"Now think carefully," asked George. "Was there signs of a fight or a struggle, or was the mess the result of someone just being a vandal? Perhaps after killing Sam."

Moishe thought hard for a while and slowly said. "Now that you ask I don't think it was a struggle or a fight. I don't think Sam had a chance somehow."

"It sounds very much like this thief, but I don't think he's killed before. Mrs. Johnson was a close thing but whether he thought she was dead or not is hard to say," said George. "We may find out more tomorrow. I'll find out if the autopsy has been done and see if they'll tell us anything. If you think of anything else, no matter how insignificant you may think it is, please tell me. What did you do after you found him?"

"I managed to get outside before I threw up. There was a phone booth at the corner so I went there and called the police. It took them about 10 minutes to get there. Even so I was still in a terrible state even after the 10 minutes. I showed them in and stayed outside. Why would God allow anyone do something like that to anyone? Does your belief in Christianity have an answer to that?"

"That's a very good question, I don't know if I understand well enough to even attempt to answer it," I said. "At a time like this nothing seems to help. We tend to think God has abandoned us. Bad things do happen all the time. The Devil is always looking for ways to separate us from God. You know firsthand, you came through the holocaust. Why did that happen? I don't understand God's ways, they are above my wisdom. I'm not sure of the exact words but it says in Isaiah 55 verses 8 and 9," 'The Lord says, my thoughts are not like your thoughts, your ways are not like my ways. Just as the heavens are higher than the earth, so are my ways higher than your ways, and my thoughts are higher than your thoughts,' "Also in Isaiah it says 'when we pass through deep waters, God is always with us.' "It says in Isaiah as well Chapter 41:10" 'Fear thou not; for I am with thee: be not dismayed; for I am thy God: I will strengthen thee; yea, I will help thee; yea, I will uphold thee with the right hand of my righteousness.'

"Some people can do just about anything to others. They have no respect for themselves or other people either," observed George. "I know I asked before but you were very upset at that time, so I'll ask again. Did Sam have any enemies? Did he owe anybody any money, even from before he moved here? Think carefully."

"I never heard of him either owing money or having enemies from now or previously," said Moishe slowly. "There is, I guess his nephew. He was always after Sam to give him money. Sam had, as you know, just given his sister half of what he got out of Switzerland. I think also that he left her everything in his will."

"Money is a powerful motive," said George. "I've seen people killed for a sum that wouldn't last the average household a month. There is an old saying in homicide "follow the money". I think the police will want to interview you again. Bring up this point about the nephew. They'll check his alibi, if he has one. You have to realize as well that you are going to be a suspect also. You found him. You are his friend. They might think you had a reason to do it. What is this nephew's name?"

"His name is Aaron Penner," Moishe said. "Och why would anyone think I would kill him he was my closest friend. We came through the concentration camp together. He worked for me. That thought is ridiculous."

"We know that," soothed George. "But the police don't know you or him. Can we think of anything else? We are close to this and must do our best for Sam. Moishe, I know you live alone and were working on your accounts Saturday. Where were you Sunday? We don't know the time of death yet, but maybe we can find out. If it was Sunday or even late Saturday then, you will need an alibi."

Robert arrived about then. He had been told by the golf club manager about our failure to be there for golf. He had tried the police station, then my place. We had to retell the whole mess. He was shocked. We all sat and thought. We discussed other reasons and could think of nothing logical. Nor could we think of anyone else who might be a suspect. It was well past lunch time, but none of us felt hungry. George pointed out that the best remedy for shock was calories. After some discussion we decided to go to the diner and eat something. A nice hot drink at least. We agreed not to discuss anything while we were there. It had to be the thief we concluded everything pointed that way. The mess, the stolen goods. The violence, everything.

The evening newspapers were full of news of the murder. The police were quoted as saying that time of death was around 11 P.M. Saturday night. They also said he had been knocked unconscious before dying. Poor Moishe, he had no alibi.

I ate an early breakfast Tuesday and went to Moishe's house to be moral support. George and Robert arrived shortly after. The police phoned to see if they could have a talk. We waited and when they arrived they asked us to leave so they could have some privacy. We told Moishe we would go to the diner and to come thereafter. The interview lasted nearly an hour. Sam's lawyer called during the interview. Moishe was named as Sam's executor. The lawyer had set up an initial interview for Friday morning.

Moishe arrived at the diner very upset at everything. George immediately bought him a piece of apple pie with cheese, his favorite and explained that sort of thing was good for distress. The police had put him through the veritable wringer. He was certain they had only gone back to the station to get permission to charge him. George didn't think so. He told Moishe that it was too early for that, they were just testing him to see if he contradicted himself. Besides they had a lot of other avenues to explore.

"Did you mention about the nephew," asked George.

"Yes," said Moishe. He appeared too rattled to continue.

"Did the police ask about him?"

"Yes, they didn't know about him and seemed very interested. They asked where he lived. I told them as much as I knew about him," brightened Moishe. "They also wrote down Sam's lawyer's number and talked to him briefly so they could go see him this afternoon."

They'll want to know the details of the will," George said. "They are bound to talk to young Penner and see if he has an alibi. You see don't you that there is no way they can arrest you now. There is still the robber to consider as well. The newspapers said the robber generally struck on Saturday nights."

We retired to my veranda were we spent the rest of the day discussing things. Mrs. MacGregor was at her best, keeping us in drinks and snacks. She did say that she had felt an evil presence on Saturday. She had, but I pointed out that could have been anything.

She hadn't been specific enough. She went off in a minor huff at that point, but rallied later with more drinks and snacks. When the time came George and I went off to the church for Bible study, where we had to go over everything again for the people there. Everyone had read the papers and were totally shocked at the worst murder hereabouts in many years.

I slept better that night. Bible study and singing hymns always soothed my soul.

Moishe called early wanting to know if I could come over for a while. Young Aaron Penner had called the night before wanting to know when he could get some money. Moishe had told him that he had no idea when that might be. He had also told him he still didn't even know what was in the will. There might not have been anything left directly to him. He told Aaron he should call the lawyer. Aaron had called the lawyer he said, and been told by the lawyer only that he had to wait for the reading and that Moishe was the executor. Moishe had said the will would be read to everyone after the funeral and not before. Aaron had insisted he be given some money and generally made a nuisance of himself. All Moishe could say was he had nothing to give him and didn't know if there was anything for him. Moishe needed some additional moral support. He, like many of us, knew little of these things. George arrived a little later he felt deeply the hurt experienced by Moishe and wanted to help. Fortunately we were there when Aaron called again. George took the phone as soon as we were aware of who it was. He told the fellow in no uncertain terms, that Moishe had no information, and to call Sam's lawyer if he wanted to know about the will. He also told him that if he harassed Moishe further we would be talking to the police.

"He's a very persistent fellow," remarked Moishe.

"Yes, I wonder why?" replied George. "We all need cheering up, let's call Robert and go to that new Italian restaurant for supper. I understand the pasta is great."

Neither Moishe nor I had eaten Italian cooking before. This was a very welcome diversion from the happenings. The food was great. There was even a small band playing Italian music. Altogether a fine way to spend the evening.

Chapter 5

John called on Friday to see if I was coming to the track to see my horses run. I said I would be there and would ask the others. Moishe would not go near the place and Robert and George opted to keep him company for the evening. The police had spent the day interviewing all of us. We were the last people to see Sam alive. The detective in charge had been sent from Toronto to head up the team and turned out to be an acquaintance of George's. Since George knew him I guessed the questioning went easier than it normally would have. Still the questioning was nothing to look forward to.

John arrived with the horses. I asked if they had traveled well and what was their general health.

"Betty's Dream, your slow coach mare has traveled well as has Dorset Lightening. They should be ready to do their best," replied John. "Of course Dorset Lightening has the best chance, but Betty's Dream is in as good shape as she'll ever be."

"We can only watch and see. Which races are they in?"

"Betty's Dream is in the first, Dorset Lightening in the seventh, then the horse you have a claim in on is in the eighth."

"I had almost forgot about that. I've had so much more on my mind lately," I exclaimed. "Yes, I'm looking forward to that as well."

The first race was a disaster from Betty's Dream's stand point. She started slowly and faded completely out of the picture. She kept gamely on, and wound up last by 8 lengths but was not any threat to any of the lowly horses in this race. I thought to myself, 'What to do with her, she has decent breeding, but no speed. I don't like putting any horse down, besides she is in the pink of health.' Then I remembered that John was taking a small step into breeding and training from scratch. Why not give it a try. It would only cost a little more. She should be given her chance.'

John and I got together after the race. "You can see now what I mean," said John.

"Yes, it's always a disappointment. Her breeding is good. She's just not cut out for it. I don't like sending horses to the glue factory and dog meat producers. Let's rest her for a while and talk about it," I replied.

John just shook his head. He's not sentimental about horses like I am. He headed for the stable to look after Betty's Dream and prepare Dorset Lightening. I headed to the club house in search of a coffee. I sat sipping my coffee as from behind me I heard someone say. "How are you tonight Ron," It was Harry White the race track manager. "I saw your mare in that first race. She didn't do very well!"

"You're being kind. She was terrible," I retorted.

"She's such a good looking horse as well," he said. "Good breeding as well as looks. Just has no speed. It happens sometimes. I see you have a claim in on Kingston Kenny in the eighth. He's a good horse. The owner only likes two and three year olds. He likes to go after the big purses. Likes to brag about how he has these great horses. You should get the horse, no other claims yet."

"Thanks," I said. "I've had my eye on him for a while. Didn't his current owner at least consider him for breeding purposes?"

"He only wants top notch racing horses. He's not into breeding. Kingston Kenny won against some of the best but not consistent enough for him," Harry replied. "Gotta go, it's a race night. Always something to see to. See you around."

Our driver took Dorset Lightening out to an early second place, we were passed on the backstretch the first time. The second horse went by as we passed the grandstand on the first circuit. This left us in fourth place as we straighten out down the backstretch for the last lap. Then not wanting to be boxed in our driver pulled out to make our run. Being on the outside on the last bend, we didn't gain on the leader. He had been leading from the start and was now tiring. We now had the second place horse boxed in on the rail with the third place ahead of us but on the outside. Turning into the final straight, Will went three wide and passed the third place horse. The second place horse started to fade and we were gaining on the leader all the way to the wire. The leader had won, but second place was very good at this higher class. Certainly no disgrace, as John was fond of saying. John joined me at the rail as Dave and Will led Dorset Lightening to the backstretch, to cool him off and get him ready to ship home.

"He's not out of his class at this level," commented John. "I can see him winning it may even be next time out. He had to go on the outside, three wide at one point. Still a good purse this time. Let's go up in the grandstand to watch the horse you have a claim on run. He should easily win here. He's certainly the class of this field. If he does win here we'll have to run him in the top conditional races from here on for a while at least. I think he's good enough to win there as well."

Dorset Lightning had won almost enough in the past two races to keep himself in food and training for about 5 or 6 months. He was truly an asset costing me very little. A joy to own. It was a shame, Betty's Dream was only a liability. Many horses just didn't have it in them.

Kingston Kenny took the lead at the start of the race and stayed there wire to wire. A clear winner. He didn't even seem to be breathing hard when he returned to the winners circle. We went to claim him. The owner wasn't even there just the groom and trainer. The trainer was sorry to see him go, but knew that his owner would be buying new yearlings to replace him.

"As I thought. This boy is going to give you some top wins. He'll have to be in the best class we have here, or you could ship him to Toronto or elsewhere to try him in higher from time to time. He'll be the top horse in the barn," said John as we headed to the back stretch with our new horse. We made arrangements to have the track keep Kingston Kenny until the next day. John would pick him up the next morning. His trailer only held two horses and would be full on the way home tonight. While making these arrangements a man came in to the office, dressed in a security guard's uniform. He spoke about some security arrangements with Harry.

Harry turned to me and introduced his security agent. "This is Kurt Mueller, one of our security people," said Harry. "He's been with us about 10 years."

"Pleased to meet you," I said, "I remember seeing you the other night."

"Thank you," replied Kurt. "It's good to meet you, I've seen you around many times as you are usually here with your horses that are racing. I think you claimed a good one tonight."

"Well I hope so," I replied. "Race horses are hard to pick sometimes, but this one does indeed look good."

"I wish you good luck with him."

"Thank you, your English is very good, were you born here in Canada?"

"No, I was born in Germany and was brought here as a prisoner of war, to a camp near Oshawa, when the war was over I asked to stay here. The people are very nice. I've been here about 10 years now."

The German people, and I had met many, were very nice ordinary hard working people, like people everywhere. The Nazis had been fanatics, including most of the prison guards. When I was a prisoner we had fared much better than Moishe and Sam, who had been used for hard labour and starved into the bargain. They had survived only because they had been young and strong when they were rounded up.

John and I decided to have a coffee to celebrate so we headed to the lounge. John had a beer, coffee for me. We talked about the possibility of breeding Betty's Dream, but reached no decisions. Since I could afford to keep her without her racing that is what would probably become of her. I could even leave her with John, at his place. It was summertime after all and even though John had limited barn space, there was plenty of room in the pastures.

Saturday and Sunday were quiet. No one felt like having our after church dinner and games. The mood was very somber. John retrieved Kingston Kenny from the track and reported he had come through the race very well. He had eaten up his feed. He wanted to know how I wanted to proceed with his training. I told him to keep him going on a regular regime and we would maybe race him again in two weeks. That met with John's approval.

Sunday I was so distracted I forgot to look at the bulletin to see if the secretary had made any goofs. The pastor delivered a super sermon, powerful, as well as soothing for our loss of a companion. It rained all day Sunday. Monday nobody was in a mood for our regular golf game. All of us felt somber and in no mood for doing much of anything. Moishe had yet to reopen the shop so we just hung around the diner drinking coffee and talking. The police called Moishe to tell him they had released Sam's body. Moishe called Sam's sister in Toronto and everything was set up to have a funeral on Thursday at the synagogue. The will to be read to the beneficiaries at three that day. Moishe wasn't needed for a couple of days so we went to my cottage on Pigeon Lake to spend the time. A little fishing and relaxing was the plan. The last few hours were consumed by our plans to go the next morning.

Early morning found us on the way. Robert and George in the back seat. Moishe in the front with me. The trunk was filled with supplies. We took our time and in about an hour arrived and unloaded the car. It was a beautiful day. George and Robert set off in the boat. For their favorite fishing spot. Moishe and I set up the cottage. The fishermen were back by eleven thirty with a pickerel and some good sized crappies. Pan fish were quite good eating. We had these for lunch cooked just in butter, pepper and salt. Moishe declared they were the best he had ever tasted. I always maintain there is nothing like fresh caught fish. We lazed our way through the afternoon. Nothing stirring on the lake. It was early season yet, the kids not out of school, mid-week and few people around. Our supper consisted of bacon, canned beans and bread sent by Mrs. Macgregor, cooked by myself. Maybe Mrs. MacGregor was right I thought, not much of a repast.

As evening set in we headed out to the lake again. It was like a sheet of glass, no wind, not a ripple except what we made. Robert and Moishe in the power boat. George and I in the canoe. They were going to troll. We would still fish, just drifting with the slight breeze. It was quite late when we returned to the dock. Robert and Moishe assisting us the last little way. They had caught a nice size walleye and we several more pan fish. We would have them for lunch the next day.

We settled back to chat for a little while.

"Things certainly haven't been dull lately," said Robert. "Why would anyone be so cruel as to kill Sam? He was a thoroughly kind gentle soul?"

"You can never tell what motivates people to kill," replied George "I've known people to kill for an amount of money that wouldn't buy a cup of coffee and a donut."

"Do you think it might have something to do with that nephew?" I asked Moishe.

"I don't know," He said "I'm just too numb to think."

"It looks to me more like the work of that burglar that's hitting people's houses," said George.

"I agree," said Moishe. "That nephew is too lazy to do anything but complain."

"Sam must have caught the robber in the act," I said. "He is most definitely violent enough."

We listened to the late news on the radio. Nothing was of much interest, there was a story about the new Major Junior A hockey team that Peterborough would be getting in the fall. They would be called the Pete's. They had played last year in Kitchener as the 'Canucks or Green shirts'. We discussed buying some tickets to see them. It would help to pass the winter. We generally didn't fish in the winter. Sitting in sub-zero weather in the middle of a lake didn't appeal to any of us. There wasn't a television here and nobody felt like playing games of any sort. We talked about having a TV but nobody was in favor of it. None of us watched TV much and it would certainly disturb the tranquility of the cottage.

However it was a good thing the veranda was completely screened, the mosquitoes and black flies being very bad at this season. We took ourselves to bed. It had been a peaceful, satisfying day.

Wednesday dawned bright and fair. We breakfasted on bacon, beans, eggs, toast, jam and coffee. Mid-morning we got the launch out and drove slowly around part of the lake. It was still very calm and tranquil. A quiet time, this was doing a world of good for our peace of mind. There were a couple of new cottages on the lake. It was a popular lake, many people from Toronto having discovered it and they were adding to the growing population. At noon we were back to the cottage were we lunched on our catch from the previous night. We packed up and headed back for Peterborough. The funeral was tomorrow.

Rain was softly descending on Thursday morning, in the kind of drizzle that looked to keep up all day. The service was nice and afterward we took the trip to the graveyard. Three o'clock found us at Sam's lawyer's office to hear the will. There wasn't too much to it. Everything was left to his sister. Her son, Aaron Penner felt he should have been left something in his own right and made an ugly scene, but his mother finally got him settled down. Wills always brought out the greed in people, but even so, he seemed rudely persistent.

Robert, George and I took Moishe to our Italian restaurant for supper. Moishe was upset but slowly coming out of it. After all the time and hard usage in the concentration camp, he was still visibly upset that Sam should have died this way. The peace of the last two days at the lake had helped a lot, he said. He thanked each of us for being such good friends and said that after dinner he just wanted to go home and be alone.

On Friday John called to say one of his horses was running on Saturday, if I was interested in coming to watch. He also apologized. It seemed that my mare had been in the next paddock to Kingston Kenny, they hadn't noticed but she had come into heat and Kenny had jumped the fence and serviced her. I had a good laugh. I told him I didn't blame him for the result, but that it was perhaps an act of God. Now we knew what was to take place in the near future for Betty's Dream. He was more upset at the stamina it had taken out of Kingston Kenny. I laughed and told him that if Kingston Kenny couldn't recover in a week, he would never be worth much. The new foal would kick off John's plan to expand into breeding. The foal, when it arrived would at least have decently good breeding, even if its mother couldn't win a race even if she started an hour before post time. We went to the races even though I had nothing running. It was a pleasure to watch such magnificent animals trying to be the leader of the pack. Saturday's race was totally uneventful. John's horse had run an even race and wound up fourth. We had forgotten about a runner he had going for Jake Sheldrake, a horse by the name of Sim's Delight, it won its race, a mid to high range claimer. That was a bonus, as Jake Sheldrake would be pleased. John had a winning streak going, this would hopefully bring new owners. There were always a few who jumped from trainer to trainer depending on who was winning.

Unknown to us the burglar stuck Saturday night. A nice big house in a new subdivision had been targeted. The young couple with their children had been away at relatives for the weekend. A neighbour had seen a small pickup truck driving away and had gone to investigate, only to find the lock of the back door broken and when opened had revealed the usual mess. He had called the police. The police had found smashed furniture in addition to the usual mess of everything dumpable on the floor. There was flour, sugar, garbage mixed with milk, juice, smashed eggs and anything else that could be emptied from the fridge. The dining room set had been broken. All the clothes had been scattered from the closets and drawers. The couple's bed had even been jumped on and broken in two pieces. The police even found the violence to be excessive. It certainly appeared that whoever the perpetrators were they enjoyed violence.

Chapter 6

Sunday's sermon was a good one. Our secretary had been up to her old tricks. This time the bulletin read "The Fasting & Prayer Conference includes meals." I don't know how she did it but she always managed something humorous. It wasn't intentional, but she didn't seem to have much of an appreciation for humor.

The week began with Robert and George wanting to go to the driving range before our golf game. We concentrated harder this time, going slowly and trying, with the help of each other, to correct mistakes. It went very well. The golf game after lunch did as well. We all shot games in the low 90's. This was a large improvement over previous results.

The newspapers on Tuesday all carried articles on a particularly brutal beating in Toronto. A person by the name of Aaron Penner had been badly beaten and wasn't expected to live. We wondered if this was Sam's nephew. Later at the diner, Moishe confirmed it. He had many broken bones. As well as internal injuries. It looked like a gangland beating.

"Well doesn't it say in the Bible, 'Never a borrower or a lender be,'" said George.

I laughed. "No, it is a quotation all right, but from Shakespeare. The Bible when it says anything about that sort of thing is almost totally opposite to that saying."

"He was always trying to get money. Perhaps he owed the wrong people," ventured George as we sat at breakfast in the diner. "Sam always said he didn't like him as he was a bad person."

"He is for certain a very violent person. He was very upset when Sam's will was read. He wanted money but it was left to his mother. I don't think she gives him much. He's is old enough to be earning his own, but wastes his time gambling," said Moishe. "His excuse for the night of Sam's murder is that he was playing poker with friends. The friends have confirmed he was there all night."

George said. "Of course facts are only as useful as one permits them to be. Take the example of the fellow who was convinced he was dead. He visited his doctor with this complaint several times and the doctor was unable to convince him otherwise. Finally, the exasperated doctor demanded whether his patient would believe in the face of physical evidence that he was alive. "Of course," said the man calmly. "I'm a reasonable fellow."

"Now would you agree that dead men don't bleed?"

"Of course."

"Fine. Give me your hand," ordered the doctor. Taking a needle, he swiftly pricked a fingertip, then squeezed it until a drop of blood beaded up. He thrust it in front of the man's eyes. "Look is that not blood."

I'll be darned," said the patient after a moment's astonished reflection. "Dead men do bleed."

"That's a terrible joke, "I said, "but I see your point."

"There goes the 'follow the money' theory anyhow," sighed George.

"I have to go now," said Moishe. "I have to open the shop. I have to work while you loafers sit around drinking coffee."

After he left Robert said. "I heard one of the better trotters at the Toronto track died mysteriously on the week end. He was the favorite to win the big 'open' race on Saturday night. They are conducting an autopsy."

"Was he Norm McKenzie's horse?" I asked.

"No he wasn't but as a result a horse trained by McKenzie's won the race."

"If you have no objection," ventured George. "What do you say to another fishing trip of a couple of days, up to your cottage?"

"Sounds like a good idea," I replied, "You and Robert gather your equipment together, then come to my place and we'll hit the grocery store before we leave. We can come back Friday night or Saturday morning, as John has both my horses running Saturday.

He has his and Jake's horses running Friday, but we don't need to attend that."

"Good idea," affirmed Robert. He was an avid fisherman." We can discuss the developments in Sam's death up there at our leisure."

Robert and George arrived at my place, and we proceeded to the grocery store, to pick up supplies. We stopped in the village of Bobcaygeon to have dinner. They did a very good dinner of pork chops, mashed potatoes, fried onions and gravy, which we all found to be delicious. The cottage was as we had left it. The skies were starting to darken, night was coming on fast, so we hurriedly got the boat ready and went trolling for a couple of hours. Our luck held and we returned with a pickerel. We had to clean it indoors as the mosquitoes and black flies were still very thick and annoying. Finally we retired to bed about one A.M.

Bacon, eggs, toast, jam and lots of coffee cooked by me made up our breakfast.

"There's a nice little trout creek not far away. Why don't we go there for the morning and back here for lunch? Maybe our luck will hold." I asked.

"Sounds like fun," said George. "We haven't tried our luck with trout in a while."

The morning was spent with the three of us spread up and down the stream. George got an old boot and a waterlogged piece of wood. Robert and I were luckier; we got nothing. A successful trip of trout fishing by our standards. There were supposed to be several good trout streams around, but we had yet to find them. We needed to find out where to go to the trout. We had good tackle, just no knowledge on where to try. The pickerel would be tonight's dinner. Over a lunch of sandwiches and soft drinks we talked about Sam's murder.

"Penner having an excuse as good as that excludes him from being there," observed George. "I guess it must have been the burglar after all. He seems to be the most likely. He is certainly violent enough, and whoever did it was very violent. I hope the police get him soon. After about two weeks things seem to fade away."

"It won't fade in our memory in a hurry. I liked Sam!" said Robert. "It looks to me that the burglar is the fellow we need to concentrate on. We don't have much of a description. Mrs. Johnson can't remember much. Do you know if the police have anything better? Maybe when Sam got back from the track he walked into a burglary in progress. He left the track early, remember." We were silent for a while thinking over the possibilities. This murder hit close to home, we had all liked Sam. We were not as upset as

Moishe, they had been friends for several years and appreciated each other above anyone else.

"The burglaries for the most part happen on the weekends, usually at night. Sam left the track mid-afternoon. We are often at the track, watching the horses' race in the afternoon, but perhaps we can think of some way to keep watch, or help in other ways," I added.

"Yes, we can put our heads together that way, but I still wonder why Penner got beat up so badly. Do you think it might be related somehow?" said George. "I don't like coincidences like that. Something smells funny about that beating. The police will investigate it though. They won't just accept that it's a coincidence."

"How do you think it is connected?" I inquired.

"That's a tough one to answer. It's just that I've long since learned to look at coincidences with distrust," replied George. "On a completely different subject. I'd like to know about this Norm McKenzie fellow. He seems to crop up all the time in racing, always in a bad way, nothing ever positive about the things he seems to be around. I don't want to think what might happen to one of your horses for instance, if it stood in the way of a win for him."

"I don't know anything more about him than what we have heard and seen lately," said Robert

"I heard his name mentioned once as a good trainer that's all," I said, "particularly good with trotters."

"Let's ask John about him when we get back to Peterborough," said George, "he seems to be headed for a clash with our horses and I for one don't like the sound of it."

"Now that you mention it, neither do I," I replied, "John will know more for sure, let's ask him."

Pickerel for supper was a treat. Served with potatoes, carrots and canned corn we had a feast. "I told you I could cook a few things, contrary to what Mrs. MacGregor would have you believe. We have some nice T bone steaks for tomorrow supper after we go to the track. Mrs. MacGregor thought that we might need building up after my cooking so, we are all invited to my place and she's going to make a huge meal for us. If it's okay with all, we'll go home Friday morning and take our accumulated fish with us. I wonder if those ladies, Mrs. Wilson and Mrs. Johnson like fish, we might give them some?"

Friday morning we spent out on the lake it had turned out to be a beautiful spring day, sunny and warm, but not yet the heat to come in a few weeks. We came away with two pickerel, both medium sized. We wrapped up our frozen fish and packed the pickerel for the drive home. We started for home shortly after lunch. Mrs. Wilson we found was visiting Mrs. Johnson, sitting in her Muskoka chairs on the veranda, talking.

"What are you ladies up to today?" George asked.

"I went out to the retirement home this week, I went to visit a lady who was a good friend of the woman who died there. Another elderly lady died this week. She sickened over a short period and passed away quite suddenly. It's almost an epidemic at the place. Most of those people are in fairly good health," Mrs. Johnson replied.

The offer of fish was accepted with enthusiasm. "This is so good of you. I love a nice feed of fish," enthused Mrs. Johnson accepting a pickerel. "You have been exceptionally kind having us to Sunday lunch and now a mess of fish."

"Would you like to join us again this Sunday?" I asked. They both replied that they would love to. We took George and his equipment back to his house.

"Please don't make this invite to Sunday dinner a regular thing," pleaded George. "I like it best with just us men. I have nothing against the ladies, they're nice people, but I enjoy it more when it's just us."

"No, I won't. It just seemed polite after her comment," I said.

"She was just fishing for an invitation and you fell for it," said George.

"Well I won't make it a habit even if she suggests it again," I said. "Are we all going to the races tomorrow to see my horses run?" George and Robert both liked the races even though none of us were betters.

"We'll be there!" they replied.

John was in a high good mood on Saturday afternoon. "Kingston Kenny's race should give him a good chance for his first win at this level. His chief competition here is Samurai Warrior. Samurai Warrior doesn't have his usual driver tonight. He's won three out of the last five races here at this level. He has a problem though. The horse hates the whip. You can't use it on him. That's why he usually gets out front and opens the biggest lead he can get. Then the others in the race usually just try for second and he steals the race. We'll stay as close to him as we can without exhausting Kingston Kenny, then if we can put on any pressure in the stretch, maybe the driver will go to the whip. If he does, Samurai Warrior will fold like a cheap tent."

"Surely his barn will have warned the driver," pointed out George.

"Quite likely," said John. "Would you take the chance of losing the race by not going to the whip, if you were the driver? This driver may not believe them and if not, Bob's your uncle."

"You think it will be that easy?" said George.

"We can but try," said John.

Dorset Lightening's race started by him pulling into second place, and staying there until the final bend. At that point he pulled out to pass. The win looked to be certain. As happens sometimes he broke stride, when the leading horse tired and swerved into him down the stretch, he finished fifth. Unforeseen things happen, onward and upward as they say. The inquiry sign went up. Will who was doing our driving complained that the driver on the horse that placed first had been hitting our horse in the face with his whip when we tried to pass. The winning horse was disqualified, the track officials had seen the incident. The disqualified horse belonged to Norm McKenzie's farm.

It seemed only an instant later and it was Kingston Kenny's turn. The crowd had made Samurai Warrior the heavy favorite. The race started as predicted. Samurai Warrior surged into the lead, while Kingston Kenny was second at the first turn he was about five lengths back. The order of horses stayed that way past the grandstand the first time. In the back stretch our driver moved up a little with gentle urging, and at the stretch pole was no more than three lengths behind. He then began urging Kingston Kenny strongly with his whip. Kingston Kenny responded to the urging and came up to the rear of Samurai Warrior's buggy. The way John predicted the driver decided to go to his whip. The results were instantaneous. Samurai Warrior jumped and broke stride. He tried to jump the rail. The total field passed him with Kingston Kenny in the easy lead taking the win.

We were ecstatic, John in seventh heaven as he had also bet on our horse. We ran down to the winner's enclosure to see the driver of Samurai Warrior being chewed out by the trainer.

Even with Dorset Lightening going on a break, it was a successful afternoon. If only we could be as successful finding Sam's murderer. We went to the barns to talk to John after our last runner. When he had seen to the after race care and loading of them for home I asked, "How much can you tell us about Norm McKenzie?"

"Why him?" asked John.

"Well we seem to be running into him in several ways lately, all of them kind of suspicious."

"I don't know much about him," said John, "he's owned that farm near Norwood for a few years, He started off as a trainer with a bit of a bang, but he's got a lot bigger lately. He lives with his sister Janet. He was married when he first came here. That's about all I can tell you. I don't pay much attention to him. He's a bit stand offish."

"Has he ever had problems with the law or track officials?"

"Not that I've heard, but I don't pay much attention to that."

"Maybe you could ask around, I don't like what I'm beginning to think about him."

"Well okay if you like," said John

Once again, on Sunday our secretary came through for us with a smile. She had written "For those of you who have children and don't know it, we have a nursery downstairs."

After church we gathered at my place as usual. We had the two invited ladies with us. John was there as well as, Robert, Moishe, George and Jim. As evening came on, we decided to have some games. The ladies opted to play Euchre against Jim and John. The rest of us had a couple of rubbers of bridge, much to Robert's delight. George and I wound up against Moishe and Robert. Moishe had news for us. It was that Aaron, Sam's nephew was back as a suspect and had no alibi. The poker players were now saying they had the wrong night originally. He had no other explanation as to his whereabouts on the night of his uncle's murder. He was in big trouble debt wise, to some very bad people. His mother was going to bail him out this time, but had attached many conditions to it. Such as getting counseling for gambling and he must get a regular job. Moishe didn't think those conditions would be kept, but Aaron's mother was hopeful. Both Moishe and Robert were good bridge players and we were badly beaten. We then all watched the Ed Sullivan show. It was very entertaining and we speculated on whether or not Ed Sullivan would have that new singing sensation Elvis Presley on his show at some point. We concluded that we would have to wait and see.

After breakfast I went to the diner to see if my friends were there. Moishe was there, George as was his habit was there. Moishe said the police were pushing Penner who had survived the beating, for an explanation, but all he would say is that he had been with a married lady and refused to tell her name.

The police apparently weren't ready to charge him yet, but were close. The burglar had struck Saturday night. He had taken mostly electronics. A big television and two radios. One of the radios had been a Blaupunkt, with several short wave reception bands. This was a very expensive radio and the police were hopeful of tracing it. The house had been trashed. This seemed to be the burglar's favorite pastime. It seemed he took pleasure in messing people's houses. The police concluded he must have a car, in order to be able to carry the television set. It appeared that this was planned well in advance.

Monday morning, John's place was a beehive of activity. Due to his recent success with my horses as well as his own and Jake's, it seems another small owner wished to have him train for him as well. It was only one horse, which had just arrived, but John was feeling that prosperity was headed his way. As he said, more and more he was needing bigger and better facilities. With a four hundred acre farm, he certainly did have the room. We talked briefly about what he could do. He thought his best move would be to go and see Jim, our banker friend and talk over the situation. He owned the farm outright, no mortgages, better times seemed just around the corner.

Both Dorset Lightening and Kingston Kenny had come through the weekend's work in fine fettle. It looked as if my mare was pregnant as well. Everything looked golden. I left John and his hands to their tasks and went to the golf course for our regular game. We were all in the mid 90's, no improvement this week, but we hadn't practiced before playing. Robert was all for a Monday morning practice before we played. To keep him happy we agreed. I didn't worry about getting better. It was nice to have it happen, but I just enjoyed the walk around the course. The walk was nice by itself, but when you added in the company of good friends and good conversation, it was a package well worth looking forward to.

Tuesday at breakfast Moishe mentioned that Aaron Penner was in a rage, but holding to his story. He was on the mend and wanted out of the hospital. The police were not going to charge him with anything yet, but were pushing hard for his lady friend's name.

John was all for trying Kingston Kenny against a better class. He was for shipping him to Toronto next week end. I told him to go ahead, we would come and cheer him home. The week went slowly. Friday finally arrived so Robert, George and I went to Toronto and booked into a hotel near the track. We were excited, John and Will would be driving down early Saturday morning.

Kingston Kenny had traveled well, John was pleased. He was in against some pretty good horses, but it looked like we had a small chance. Early in the race he got boxed in and couldn't advance until the last turn. He came on with a terrific burst and wound up second. The winning time for this class looked slow, so maybe next time. The favorite hadn't run well. He looked to be asleep. A horse trained by Norm McKenzie was the winner.

It was looking more and more like this McKenzie fellow was fixing races somehow. If so it wasn't readily apparent. We needed much more information. 'I guess I'm just nosy' I thought.

Chapter 7

As we traveled home Sunday we discussed the racing on Saturday. The horses were much better than we saw in Peterborough, and the purses bigger. Kingston Kenny had won more for his second place finish than he would have got for a win at home. No wonder Norm McKenzie operated out of Toronto, much more latitude for manipulation. As well we decided to take a little fact finding trip to Norwood and see if we could subtly find out more about him. We would just ask a few innocent questions and see what was known.

Monday after breakfast at the cafe, we headed to Norwood. The cafe was on the main street which was Highway 7, easy to find. We sat down to order a coffee.

"How to begin," said Robert.

"Well let's just wait a few minutes," said George "some opportunity may present itself."

There seemed to be an altercation occurring between the waitress and a customer. The argument conclude by the customer stocking out in a bad mood. The waitress came our way to get our order but stopped at the table beside us to ask the older man seated there who the fellow was.

"He's one of Norm McKenzie's grooms, Norm McKenzie has a horse farm just outside of town. I'd stay away from that fellow though if I were you," said our neighbor, "he's bad news. He's lived most of his life here in town and he was convicted a couple of times when he was young of being cruel to animals."

"I'll keep clear of him, thanks for the advice," said the waitress. She took our order for coffee and went to fill it.

I said to the man seated at the next table, "I overheard you speak of Norm McKenzie and his racing stable. Do you know him well?"

"Nobody knows that fellow well," said our neighbor, "he keeps away from most people in town. Very hard to know. Kind of a snob. Won't talk to the common folk."

"Well I'm not sure what to do now," I said, "I had been thinking about getting a new trainer for my horse and was going to see him about it, but that doesn't sound like a good recommendation. I don't want someone I can't talk to about my horse."

"Well I don't know anything about horse racing," said our friend, "but I wouldn't hire him for anything. He has a bad reputation. I guess that's why he hires that groom that was just in here. He once had a wife, but they say he beat her. Anyway, she divorced him. Now he lives with his sister. She seems to be the only person he can get along with."

"I heard a horse died at his farm recently?" I said.

"That seems to be a regular occurrence. I don't know how so many can die in one place. The glue factory truck is a regular visitor. That's another reason I wouldn't board a horse there. We had horses for our farm work when I was young. They are magnificent creatures. Quite smart in their own way."

"I guess I better rethink my choice as a trainer."

"I think that would be wise," he said.

We finished our coffees and got back into the car. "Well we got some information which confirms what we were thinking but how to get more specific information. What we have is all circumstantial and you can't get anyone to believe something criminal is going on without something concrete," said George.

"What we need is somewhere quiet to think. Let's go to the cottage tomorrow and do a little fishing and tossing things around. We'll come up with something. We're all fairly intelligent, and we all hate a cheater," replied Robert.

We were in agreement so first thing in the morning we headed north. An hour and a half later we were in the boat heading for Nogie's Creek bay, our favorite trolling spot in the early summer. There was a steady light rain coming down. Since it was not very heavy, we persevered.

"What we could really use is a spy at McKenzie's farm. If we could get to that guy we saw at the cafe in Norwood that would be great, but he probably wouldn't help us, he probably likes what is going on and the boss probably pays him well," said George

"If we ask around we might find someone who has left that employ. Grooms move around a lot. They don't always know what is happening right under their nose, but we could get lucky," I said.

"I agree, that sounds like a good plan. Let's ask around when we get back to Peterborough, particularly we could get John to ask around the barns on the backstretch to see if we can track down someone who used to work for McKenzie, then sound him out about the situation," said Robert

"Good idea," said George, "we have to go carefully, we don't want McKenzie finding out we're asking about him, but that seems to be the best approach."

We caught two bass, so we headed back to the cottage where we relaxed for the rest of the day and let the world go by. We were all frustrated by the lack of progress in Sam's murder, so we decided that after breakfast we would brain storm on what we could do to help the police. We had a good supper of steak, potatoes and carrots, with an apple pie for dessert. Mrs MacGregor had been the pie manufacturer but I did the cooking. I got teased but also told it was a success.

To open our discussion, George said. "The police won't like us interfering in any way in their investigation. We need to do things that won't get in their way. I'm stumped at what to suggest."

"Well you're the expert, but I wonder if they would object to us cruising in our cars around likely neighborhoods on Saturday nights?" I speculated.

"I don't think that would create a problem," said George. "The burglaries all seem to be shortly after midnight until early morning. We could start after the races on Saturdays and try it for a couple of weeks. After the races we could have an early nap, then we would be reasonable fresh for the patrol. We would need some way to communicate though."

"Sounds okay to me," added Robert. "If you have no objections I'll set up the patrol areas. I have a new map of the city. I'll get two more and we'll mark them off."

"Good thought," said George.

"It doesn't look like young Penner is involved with the burglaries. For one thing he was in hospital for the last few days. That doesn't mean he didn't kill Sam. We could get Moishe in on this and have him contact Sam's sister to gossip every few days. This should help keep tabs on Penner and what is happening on that front."

We kicked around several other minor ideas, but these seemed to be the best we could come up with just now. We went for a swim. The water was beautiful. The day was bright with hardly a cloud in the sky. Even the mosquitoes stayed away. We did a little fishing in the evening, caught a pickerel and a Muskie in a very short time, so we called it a night and went back to the cottage. It had been a very quiet, relaxing day. We were physically removed from Sam's murder and the robberies and felt more peaceful.

At breakfast I opened the subject, which had been on my mind for a couple of weeks. "What do you two say about staying up here most of the summer? None of us really needs to be stuck in the city. We could go down Friday mornings, pick up what we need, go to any races that John has set up, do a patrol Saturday night, stay at home for the night, go to church Sunday morning and come back here Sunday afternoon. It's only about an hour's drive. We could fish, swim and generally have a relaxing summer. If we need to do any research on the McKenzie question we could stay for a few hours or even a day."

George was the first to reply after they had both had a think about the proposition. "I could, the only thing is I wouldn't have time to do much around the house."

"You could get Mrs. Wilson from across the street to do a bit of cleaning and perhaps the laundry once in a while. I don't know if you could afford her say once a week, but think about it. She could use a little extra money. It's not as if you have much to do with the lawn and garden. For that matter I could get my man to cut your grass as necessary. The same with you Robert."

"We would find it a bit difficult doing most of our laundry here," Robert pointed out.

"It may shock you to know, that I've been thinking about that too," I said. "I've wanted a washing machine, dryer and even a shower here for a while. I was thinking of going into town today to order them. A hot water tank as well of course. I might as well order a phone line while I'm at it. Then we could be in touch with the outside world."

"You may regret that one," put in George. "The outside world has a way of intruding on your peace if you let it."

"Let it intrude, I need to talk to Mrs. MacGregor once in a while as well as John. I need the convenience," I replied.

We finished breakfast and ran into Bobcaygeon. I ordered the washer, dryer, and water heater and arranged for the plumber to install them the following week. Thankful that he was not too busy to do the job, I headed for the nearest phone. I got the phone promised for installation on the next Monday. While in the phone booth I called John to see if we had anything of mine racing

Saturday afternoon, and found that Dorset Lightening was set to go, so I told him we would be there to watch.

"You know," said George, "the more I think about it we need a way to keep in touch with each other while on patrol. The army surplus store must have some mobile communication units that were used in the war. If the budget allows we should get three. We all learned to use them in wartime. They would help us keep track of what is happening and come to each other's assistance if needed."

"Good idea, we'll stretch the budget to include them. We'll go a wee bit earlier Friday and see if the local surplus store has some," I replied.

We went to Peterborough on Friday in a kind of euphoria. Everything went smoothly. We told the police of our plan and asked if they would mind us doing the patrols. The police said they were okay with that so long as we stayed out of the way, and to call them immediately if we saw something suspicious. They had no solid leads on the burglar or Sam's murder. Moishe was grateful for our efforts to track down Sam's killer and promised to keep a line of communication with the Penner's. Sam's murder had hit us all hard, Neither Robert nor I had been that close to a murder before. We got our radios from the war surplus with two extra batteries each. Lunch was in the Italian restaurant, the lasagna was superb.

We then headed for the track. Even Dorset Lightning was on to his game and won by a neck after leading from wire to wire with no serious challenges.

We took a short rest at home then at midnight we did our first patrol. We cruised the streets until dawn but none of us saw anyone suspicious or otherwise. The radios worked to perfection.

We went home for a couple hours of rest before church. The secretary had been humorous again, she had written "For an 'in memoriam' offering please place your donation in the envelope along with the deceased person you want remembered." She hadn't let us down.

We had a talk with John on the way north. He had entered Dorset Lightning in the top race for Saturday, along with his two and one of Jake Sheldrake's horses. He also told us that he had bought a bigger horse trailer, and bought lumber to start on a new barn for 10 more horses. Things were looking up for John. Will, Dave and himself would be the builders. They were all handy with tools and had done similar things before.

"Do you know anyone who used to work for Norm McKenzie and doesn't anymore? Is there anyone at all that has quit there or been fired that you know of?

"Boy, you really have a thing about this McKenzie fellow don't you!" said John. "What did he ever do to you?"

"Nothing yet, that I know of at least, but I worry about what he may be up to, it looks as though that he will any day now. There is little doubt in my mind that he is manipulating races. I was kind of upset when that horse of his went berserk and got shot. It got my dander up."

"Well I don't know anyone, but grooms generally move around a lot. I'd be surprised if there wasn't several around. I can ask around if you like."

"Please do that, but be careful, I don't want him to hear about us inquiring."

Our neighbor from four cottages further along the road was walking his dog, as we pulled into the lane Monday afternoon. He came over to talk. He had just come to the cottage for the summer.

"Was your place broken into last winter?" were his first words.

"Not that I noticed," I replied. "Did you have problems?"

"Yes, we lost just about anything of value. I've reported it to the police, they have been out and fingerprinted the whole place. I don't know if they got anything, but the burglars sat in the cottage, lit a fire in the fireplace, and drank several beers. They left the empties, so we can hope," he said.

"I was up several times over the winter. I like cross country skiing. It's good around here in the winter," I said. "I never noticed anything."

"Apparently the police have a couple of other break-ins, not on this lake but close by. People who are not here in the winter," he continued.

This was not good news, there seemed to be burglars all over the place.

"Was there any other damage, such as furniture overturned or things like flour, dishes or that sort of thing strewn around," put in George.

"No, nothing of that nature," he replied.

Later that day the telephone man installed our new phone. We fished and relaxed. Wednesday our new washer, dryer and hot water tank arrived. While the plumbers were busy installing those we went to town and had a game of golf. The course was not very challenging, but we had a good time anyway. Thursday we fished our trout stream but had no luck, and afterward took turns washing our clothes in the new machines. We discovered that despite our watch the previous Saturday, the burglar had struck again. We called Moishe and found out the police had given up on all other avenues to find Sam's murderer. Moishe said that a lady had come forward to say she had been with Penner. He had got a new alibi.

"I think what we need here is a cleaner for the cottage, she can do the washing and general cleaning, maybe two days a week. That'll keep the place here nicer as well. What do you think?"

"It's your money," said George.

"Sounds okay to me," echoed Robert.

"I'm going into town to see about a cleaner, right after breakfast. Would you two like to come or you can stay here and do what pleases you? Fishing, swimming, relaxing anything you wish."

"I'm not interested in town just now," replied George. "I think I'll go drown some worms."

"Fishing sounds good to me as well," said Robert.

I made up a little notice for the bulletin board in the grocery and headed to Bobcaygeon. Mrs. Jackson, the owner of the grocery, met me at the door. In answer to my question about putting up the notice I had made. She asked if she might make a suggestion. I told her I would welcome any suggestion. She suggested young Mary Keifer. Mrs. Keifer was raising Mary and a younger brother on a limited income. She told me Mrs Keifer's husband had been killed in the war. (This war had cost a lot of innocent people a tremendous amount, both in Europe as well as everywhere else including in Japan and Germany). Mary had told her she always wanted to be a doctor but there was no money to send her on to school. She would be entering her last year of high school in the fall. Mrs. Jackson explained that Mary had lowered her sights to be a nurse, but that still required more money than they were likely to be able to afford. I asked where I might find this person and Mrs. Jackson directed me to the post office. Mrs. Keifer worked there. Mrs. Keifer was a pleasant, smiling individual who I took a liking to immediately. I explained my mission. She was interested and thought her daughter would be interested as well. She wasn't sure were her daughter was at present, but I said I wasn't in a terrible hurry. I explained the job, two days a week, general cleaning, clothes washing, dishes, dusting and vacuuming. She said she thought her daughter would be pleased with the offer as she couldn't find another job around. I set up an interview for the next day, very pleased at the way things were going.

I returned to the bulletin board in the store. There was an advertisement for a handyman looking for work. He had listed brickwork as one of his skills. I called him from the phone booth and found him home and able to build me a barbecue. He had done a couple before and could start right away. I hired him. I had been thinking that a barbecue might be a nice addition.

My sons were coming to visit on the weekend so George and Robert decided they would go to Peterborough for Friday night and come back Monday morning.

The handyman arrived the next morning and set to work. He had brought the fixins' so to speak. Bricks, mortar, tools and even a grill were unloaded. George was busy all morning with

99

a "secret" project, which he presented mid-afternoon. He had taken a handheld outdoor camping toaster and modified it so we could barbecue fish. It certainly sounded like a good idea. I had never had barbecued fish. We could hardly wait till the barbecue was finished. The handyman said it would be completed the next afternoon, but would need at least a day to cure properly. We decided to get the fish. With that in mind we retired to our trout stream and managed to catch four good big trout. Those were the first we had ever caught in that stream.

George and Robert went after bass the next morning. I headed to town to interview our prospective cleaner. She proved to be as nice and down to earth as her mother. I told her that we needed her two days a week and asked if Tuesday and Thursday were good for her. She said they were and thanked me. I asked if she wanted more work, I told her I could talk to a neighbor and find out if they might fill out her week for her. She was moved and said she would be glad of anything. We talked about her plans for further education and she told me all about her hopes. I told her I used to be a school teacher, and how good it was to hear young people so enthusiastic. We talked about transportation and she said her grandfather had an old car that worked fairly well. I asked her to come Thursday to start and I would show her what I wanted done. I said if her grandfather's car broke down, just to call and I'd come for her. I told her to bring her bathing suit if she wanted to, as the beach was good. A dip after work I felt would feel good. Food was no problem I said as there was always plenty in the fridge and she could make herself anything she wished.

That chore settled I returned to the cottage for some lunch, a swim and perhaps a little fishing. In the evening when we gathered on the veranda.

Robert said. "We have so many fish we were going to have to open a store to sell them."

"You know," I replied. "That's not a bad idea, we could have a barbecue and invite the neighbors to it. We could barbecue a few fish, if that turns out to be a good method of cooking them, and also have hot dogs and hamburgers as a supplement. We could all use a little party to relax. What do you two think of that idea?"

"I think it's a great idea," said George. "When could we do that?"

"We could forgo our patrol, particularly if it's not turning anything up and have it Saturday afternoon. Not this weekend but the long weekend. This weekend is taken by my sons' visits. I stayed at the cottage Friday while George and Robert went south to do a Saturday patrol.

They later told me Saturday Dorset Lightning ran very badly and afterward had a bad case of diarrhea. The vet said it must have been something he ate or drank. Will reported seeing one of McKenzie's grooms near our stall. McKenzie's horse had won.

The patrol was no more fruitful than the previous week end. At one point George thought he might have seen a suspicious looking pickup truck cruising around, but the truck had sped up and left the area. Robert had seen nothing. The newspaper had got the story of our doing patrols and requested an interview. Robert directed them to me and told them it was my idea, but I was at the cottage with my family for the weekend. John called Sunday afternoon to tell me they had located a couple of ex-employees of McKenzie's operation.

I called George and asked that he and Robert remain in Peterborough as I would come down with my son when they were headed home. I wanted to talk to these ex-employees on Monday if I could track them down.

The reporter called about 9:00A.M. Monday to ask for an interview. He was excited that someone cared enough to try a little harder.

"What made you and your friends come up with this idea," he asked.

"The police have enough to do without spreading their force even thinner with neighbourhood patrols," I said "We thought that at least we would keep it fresh in our memories by doing something about it. It was a very cruel murder of our friend and we don't want it dropped. The police have run out of leads. This burglar that's in the news just now is a violent person, but there is nothing else to link him or them if it's more than one person, to Sam's murder, We just felt if we could get one crime solved it might help to clear the air."

"Was there anything that made you think of these burglars as the killer of your friend?"

"Not anything concrete but the two incidents happened around the same time. Then too, how many violent crooks are around at the same time," I said

"Well I wish you good luck, we don't need the burglaries let alone murder happening in our fair city," he said.

After he asked several other minor questions and when he was satisfied that he had all the details he left.

Chapter 8

John had found out that two grooms who had worked for McKenzie were called Shamus O'Sullivan and Henry Jones. O'Sullivan had since taken a job with a trainer who worked at the St. Catherine's track. He had seen Jones around the backstretch on Saturday bumming money from his fellow grooms. John didn't know where he lived, but thought he was living rough around town. He thought I might find him hanging around the track. I went to the track. Jones was indeed hanging around. I offered him a coffee and donut if he would come and talk to me for a while. We went to the cafe.

"What's on your mind," he asked when we had our coffee and donut.

"I understand you used to work for Norm McKenzie," I said by way of an opener.

He immediately got very still and withdrawn. "So what's it to you"

"I just wondered what you thought of the operation," I said

"I've got nothing to say," he replied.

"Well I can understand you being cautious," I said. "I've heard some things about the place. I was thinking about sending a horse to have him train it, but I've heard rumors that make me hesitate. I don't like hearing about possible race fixing and horses dying. Things like that I'd like to stay away from if I can."

He visibly relaxed. "How do I know you're not trying to trap me into saying something against him," he said.

"You don't but I could take you to see some people and introduce you so you would have a better knowledge of me."

"Like who for instance."

"How about my friend John Smith, he's a trainer and a friend of mine, he trains my horses, but I'm going to have a runner in Toronto and I was thinking of having McKenzie look after him, while he's there."

"I know Smith," he said. "He's your trainer?"

"Yes he trains Dorset Lightning, have you seen him run? He raced a week ago."

"Yes I saw him, he won over a good field, a nice horse. He lost last time out, he looked good, I've seen that driver try that tactic before, I don't know why he bothers, and it's always spotted. Dorset Lightning would have won easily except for the interference. I tell you what I'll check you out and we can meet here tomorrow at 9:00 A.M. if you like. I just don't want any trouble from McKenzie and his crowd."

"That sounds reasonable to me," I said.

I drove out to John's farm. They were busy building the new barn, it was going to have 12 new stalls, 6 along each side. Storage for hay attached with feed and tack room inside. John left Will and Dave to continue and came over to me.

"Let's go inside have a cool drink and talk," he said, "I've got a big pitcher of lemonade for our breaks."

When we were seated with a drink in hand, I said. "I found that Jones fellow and talked to him briefly. He was cautious about what he said, but I think he has a lot to tell. He wouldn't say more but wanted to check me out before proceeding. We're going to meet again tomorrow."

"I don't know much about him, myself," said John. "He seems honest enough, as far as I know he doesn't even drink, that's unusual in a groom. McKenzie bad mouthed him when he quit there. I guess just the fact that he quit and wasn't fired speaks well of him. I've never needed to hire any drifters so I don't know much about the breed."

"I've got a proposition for you," I said, "what would you say to let me take Dave away from you for a while."

"Hold on," said John, "I need him worse now than when I hired him."

"You didn't let me finish. What I want to propose is this. I would like to have someone I trust looking after Kingston Kenny while he's racing in Toronto. He could keep a covert eye on McKenzie and staff, without getting involved or making a thing about it. He's intelligent, we could lend him to the trainer you're using in Toronto. He could get experience working for a different trainer at the same time. I would pay his salary, room, board and expenses. That would give us some better security for Kingston Kenny and kind of spy on McKenzie at the same time. They would think nothing about having a new groom around. They wouldn't be looking for something like that either."

"I need him here," said John, "we're busier now than we can handle!"

"I know, but that's just the first part. This Jones fellow needs a job. You could offer him the job. That would give him a nice warm fuzzy feeling about us. Maybe we could get a lot more out of him as a result. When I talk to him tomorrow, I could suggest to him to come see you."

"I guess it could work, I've never heard anything against Jones and if things keep going the way they are I'll probably need someone else shortly. It would give me a chance to look him over."

"That's the spirit, I'll mention it tomorrow then, but we better get Dave's okay first."

"I'll call him in and we'll put it to him."

John called Dave in to the house, when he was seated with a
coffee, I said. "Dave we have a proposition to put to you. You don't
have to accept it. It would have no impact whatsoever on anything.
Here's what we propose. Temporarily you would move to Toronto
while Kingston Kenny is running there. You would look after him
only. You would work for the trainer there and learn how he does
things, but we would pay your room, board, expenses and salary.
While you are there I would like you to very carefully keep an
eye on Norm McKenzie's grooms, or any of his other employees
and watch what happens in races the horses he trains or owns are
running. That part you don't have to do if you wouldn't like to do
that sort of thing. We do want you to watch that they don't have a
chance to do anything to our horse. We think he's manipulating
races by having horses run slower than they should, maybe even
doping them somehow. Perhaps giving them something to get them
to run faster than they ordinarily would. Anything of that sort."

"I think I'd like to do that," said Dave, "but I don't fully
understand what you want."

"I don't want them to catch you watching or anything of the
sort. If they seem to be watching you then back off completely. In
other words, ignore what they are doing. You could be in danger, I
don't want that. I will say there probably is no danger, I only have
suspicions. Your primary duty is to be Kingston Kenny's groom,

particularly watch that no one tries to feed him something or give him something to drink. That's what they may be doing to the horses that run slower and allow them to win big purses. That's what I think they're doing. Watch the races that their horses are in and see if they win when they shouldn't or lose when they should win. Do you understand?"

"I would like to see how other people train, and I'd like to see Toronto, I've never been there. I can be careful and if they ask about me watching I can say I'm learning other people's methods."

"Yes that's the idea, but be very careful, we may be dealing with very violent people here. Ok, if you'd like to try it then John will arrange with his trainer in Toronto. I have a rooming house with a vacancy or two just now so you can stay there. It's pretty basic, but should be good cover that way too. You'll have to look after your own meals and so on. We can drive you down tomorrow, show you how to get around on the streetcar system and that sort of thing."

"What about the work around here?"

"John will look after that, the operation is growing and you are a vital and much needed part of it. Kingston Kenny will be down there most of the summer I guess, but we'll keep in touch with you. I'll come down to visit now and then. I also want you to report anything to me by phone at any time. I'll pay you back for the expenses of the long distance calls and all that sort of thing. Just don't call me from the track. There is no phone at the rooming house so we'll get you setup with one, we want you to call often."

"I'll do my best but my mind will be more on Kingston Kenny than on intrigue."

"That's the way it should be, just keep your eyes open as well if you can. If not, no harm done. Get your stuff together, we'll go down tomorrow and get you set up."

Nine A.M. found me at the cafe, Jones was there as well, and that alone told that he was to be trusted to be on time at least. He hadn't eaten breakfast, I was sure he had no money so, I ordered for both of us. While we were waiting for the order I said, "Did you get a chance to find out anything about me?"

"Yes I did," he answered, "It seems you have a reputation as being a good honest sort. I'll trust what I've heard about you and try to answer your questions."

"Good, we'll eat first and talk over coffee later, if that's okay with you."

Our order arrived and we concentrated on our food. Jones seemed to be in an upbeat mood. He ate quickly, 'probably doesn't have much a good bit of the time' I thought. Finally we got to the coffee stage.

"Please excuse me for asking," he said, "but would ya be willing to pay something for me answering questions, I don't have a job right now and I don't like living off my friends all the time?"

"Yes, I'd be willing to pay you a fee, whether or not you can answer my questions," I said. "I do have a bit of a proposal for you, my trainer has an opening just now, and I asked him if I could mention it to you. He said yes, I don't do his hiring but if you present yourself to him tomorrow he'll talk to you about it."

"Thank you," he said, "I ain't been successful at gettin' a job since I left McKenzie's farm. What time should I go out to the farm?"

"I'd say if you got there about 11:00 AM it would be a good time. He'll want to talk to you and find out some of your background, just be honest with him and he'll probably hire you. It's up to him."

"Good enough for me. Fire away with your questions."

"OK, first of all can you tell me why you left McKenzie?"

"I don't like cruelty to any animal, and they quite often treated their horses cruelly. A couple of horses died while I was there and I think they were to blame. I didn't like the 'feel' of the place neither. It wasn't a very happy place."

"How did these horses die?"

"I'm not sure but I think they fed them somethin', I know one of them got real bad diarrhea and died. I heard a remark from one of the trusted grooms about somethin' in its feed. See the horse was just an old gelding too old to race, it was just there as to an old folks home. No one paid any attention because the horse was worth nothing."

"Is this what happened to the other one that died, you mentioned there were two of them?"

"I don't know, I was just told it died, it was another old gelding, of no use anymore. They always have a lot of old horses out to pasture"

"I'm with you," I said, "I don't like cruelty either, but from that we can't tell if it was a case of cruelty."

"Yes I know, but I also think they were somehow training horses to run slower than they could. I don't know how. They have a couple of grooms that are the trusted ones and they get the jobs to look after those things. One guy is real cruel. He seems to love to see animals get hurt. He's sort of the head groom. I spoke to Mr. McKenzie about him, but Mr. McKenzie just said he thought I was exaggerating but I wasn't."

"I think I've seen that fellow," I said, "Did you ever hear of them manipulating races to win or lose?"

"I heard them laughing about a race that our horse lost. They had bet on some other horse. Our horse had been leading but he broke stride. They didn't let me go to the races, just worked around the farm.

"Is there anything else that you noticed while you were there?"

"They did some funny things, now that you mention it, like putting a lot of oats in water and soaking them for a while, before drying them out again, then feeding them to a horse when they were dry. I don't know if that was anything. Horses got sick a lot at that farm, but most of them recovered okay."

"Was there something put in the water or was it just water that the soaked the oats in?"

"I don't know."

"How about the horses that were fed these oats after they were dry again, were they horses that got sick?"

"I don't know that either, I never kept track."

"How long were you there?"

"Just four months, I didn't like it because it was creepy. I haven't been able to get a job since, but I'd rather not be working there"

"We've beat this subject to death I guess, you've been very cooperative. Would $20.00 cover what you would like as a fee for your information?" I said.

"That would be much appreciated," he said. "If I get the job with Mr. Smith, I promise I'll do a good job for him."

"I certainly would appreciate it if you could, I have my horses there, and he's growing and needs good help."

We shook hands and parted. I drove out to the farm to pick up Dave to drive to Toronto. Dave was ready and anxious, we had over an hour drive ahead of us. Robert and George came along. George knew Toronto well from the years he had spent there as a detective. On the way we went over everything we wanted Dave to do. He caught on fast. The house I had for rent was on Galley Avenue, near High Park. It was a working class area. Mainly polish people, nice people. They had nice delis and stores mainly along Roncesvalles Avenue, right on a main street car route. Luckily there was a used furniture store nearby, so Robert and I went there and picked up some furniture for the apartment while George showed Dave the streetcar route to the track. While he was there he took Dave into the barns and introduced Dave to the trainer, showed him were Kingston Kenny was kept, where the feed and water was to be had. Then they took the return trip. George wrote out the instructions on how to get to and from the track and to the attractions downtown on Yonge Street. Robert and I had got him a bed, couple of chairs, small table, small radio and a light. I ordered in a phone and set up with the couple in the other unit to let the installer into Dave's unit so he could install the phone. We had picked up a few groceries to get him going. Nothing very perishable as he had no way to keep the groceries cool. All of us got in the car and drove the short distance to High Park, we walked around Grenadier pond and chatted. I told him I was putting a phone in his unit and I wanted him to call John every day and report anything at all no matter how insignificant. Finally we left Dave to his own devices and got motel rooms for the night. We would return to Peterborough on Wednesday.

Driving back the next day Robert said, "How do you think he'll make out?"

"He's by himself in a big city for the first time in his life," said George, "He's bound to have some problems, but he's quite bright. I bought him a map and told him, that he should ask people the way if he gets lost. We got a bank account set up at the bank there on Roncesvalles when we got back from the track. I put the money in it for him that you gave him as an advance. It's a better set up than most people have when they first get there."

On our return to Peterborough we drove straight to John's place to get him up to date with Dave's situation.

"We set up Dave to call every evening. I got him a phone so he doesn't have to call from a pay phone. I don't want him calling from the track in particular, he might be overheard. I hope I haven't put him in danger," I said to John.

"He's pretty smart," said John, "he'll be cautious I'm sure, he realizes the danger. He and I had a long talk Monday night. I told him of all the things I've ever heard about this business. It seems to attract a lot of crooks. That Jones fellow came out and asked for a job, he sounds good so I hired him."

"Sounds as if our plans are working out well so far. Do you have anything running Friday or Saturday?"

"I have a new owner with two horses coming in tomorrow. I'm going to need those extra stalls. A little success goes a long way sometimes. Jake Sheldrake's two horses are running Friday. Dorset Lightning still seems weak from that diarrhea so, only my mare for Saturday."

"We may skip Friday's card but God willing we'll be there for Saturday's. I'll be having our Sunday afternoon dinner as usual with a game night and maybe some TV after. Will you be there?"

"Yes I'll be there, I'll see if I can get Will to come as well. He does sometimes. I can leave the farm in charge of that Jones fellow. It'll be a good test of his trustworthiness.

"Robert, George and I will do a patrol after the races and a nap Saturday. The following week we'll be at the cottage. Call me if there is anything newsworthy from Dave."

Chapter 9

Tuesday and Wednesday we tried trolling on Little Lake and the Otonabee River, our luck wasn't with us but we managed to catch quite a few large rock bass, not the best of catches but at least something to show. These we gave to Mrs. Wilson. She said she would share with Mrs. Johnson. Even then she felt there would be enough for a couple of meals each.

As I was eating my breakfast Tuesday morning Mrs. MacGregor said, "Ever since that article in the paper about you doing patrols to help the police, I've been having bad dreams nearly every night. I see you in the hospital, badly hurt. Mr. Mackie also getting hurt."

"You say Robert is hurt in your dreams, how badly?"

"He doesn't seem to be as badly hurt as you. I can't seem to tell whether it's up at your cottage or here in Peterborough. I'm sure it's connected to these break-ins somehow, but maybe it's just my sensitive nature. I just thought I'd tell you, so you can be extra cautious."

"We intend to be very careful. It's nice of you to warn us, but I believe we'll be all right."

On Wednesday we drove out to the airport to look around. The flying bug seemed to be biting Robert and me at least. We walked to the flying club and asked about getting our licenses. We were directed to the head instructor, only to discover that he was ex-RCAF. He told us there wasn't much to be done to get our licenses, since Robert and I had been air force pilots during the war, just familiarization with the Cessna's and a check ride. He took us on a tour of the hanger and points of interest. There was a half-finished plane in one part of the hanger and we found out that a fellow in town was building it. Apparently there was a flourishing home built club. This was news to us. Robert who had been an engineer before the war was very interested. We were told that the one there at present was a Druine Turbulent. It was to be powered by a Volkswagen car engine. Amazing. First we made appointments for check ride, with Robert also getting the information on the home building club.

Thursday we went to the driving range after breakfast and then got in a golf game. George managed to shoot an 89. We teased him about going on the pro tour in a couple of weeks. Robert had a 91 and I even managed a 93. It looked like better golf bred better golf. Friday we repeated the procedure, but came away disappointed. None of us repeated Thursday's figures. We just lazed around the rest of the time, I'm good at that part. Saturday afternoon we headed to the race track. Sundown Sheila was in too high of a class and finished a tired fourth. John was satisfied with the result. He knew he had put her in a tough spot.

We left for our patrol and although we kept going until 6:00 AM none of us saw anything the least bit suspicious. The church secretary offered the only spot of humor for the weekend. The bulletin read, 'A bean supper will be held on Tuesday evening in the church hall. Music will follow.' priceless. I guess even when she proof read the Mimeograph sheet she wasn't getting the point.

Sunday dinner Mrs. MacGregor fooled us by having roast chicken instead of her usual roast beef. She rarely had chicken on the menu. It was delicious as usual, the evening entertainment went well and we were able to head to the cottage Monday, feeling very pleased with the way things were going. We had a barbecue to prepare.

Our nearest neighbor was there when we arrived at the cottage, walking his dog, anxious to tell us that two more cottages on our road had been broken into over the winter. People were nearly all up now for the duration of the summer. A few had not yet put in an appearance but we were now well into the summer. We asked him to pass the information around to everyone that we were having a barbecue to kick off the summer on Saturday. Everyone was welcome, to start around 1:00 P.M., to end whenever we fell asleep.

Even though it was a cool, windy day we went fishing for the evening, but with no luck we returned to the cottage early and spent the remainder of the evening just talking and listening to the news on the radio. The Summer Olympics had started with the Equestrian events in Sweden. The remainder would be in Australia in November. They had changed where the horse events were to be held, some problem with shipping horses to Australia. We could only hope that Canada did better than last Winter Olympics, we could only manage 1 silver and 2 bronze there. Elvis Presley had been on the Milton Berle show earlier in the month and the audience had been scandalized by his suggestive hip movements. We sat on the veranda to discuss things.

I said, "Before we get to the racing and Sam's murder I just wanted to mention that, Jim had been at church on Sunday and told me how he felt he was just sort of coming alive. He had suggested he could help with the patrols. I know how he had been feeling. I always thought getting divorced was very like having a loved one pass away."

"What do you mean by coming alive?" questioned Robert.

"He told me that he felt like he was coming out of shock. He said that was how he thought coming out of shock would feel. He's been divorced about four years now. He claims that even now he feels he loves his ex-wife. She decided that she wanted something else out of life and left him. Then divorced him. They had two children and he was in shock he felt. He never thought she felt that way. She almost immediately got a new boyfriend and settled down with him. After 20 years of marriage, he was devastated. She had obviously had no respect for him even after the 20 years together. It wasn't divorce of course with me. My parents died, then soon after my wife. It seems to me like I've sort of come out of a fog this past two months. I don't know how else to describe it. I have all this money and I'm not an extravagant person, so I think I'll give a big chunk to each of my sons. I'm also going to spend a little more on myself."

"That's interesting, I'm glad things are starting to work out for him, maybe he can join us more often," said George. "We could use more help on the patrols, if we ever encounter the crooks we're kind of outnumbered and then too, if we get in hot pursuit, we could use one person to drive and one to work the radio."

"That's a good point," said Robert, "Did you ask him if he was interested?"

"I thought we might discuss it, like now and ask him next time we're down there to patrol. He certainly has the week ends off and he was just as upset as us over Sam's murder."

"Good let's ask him as soon as we get back there, in two weeks," said Robert. "How about this racing venture are we going to get anywhere with this. I mean, don't get me wrong I don't like what's happening either, but it seems impossible to catch them red handed at anything. Even if we do what do we do then. Most people don't care much about dead animals?"

"The racing authorities could put a stop to most of it by lifting his license, and the SPCA would go after him for cruelty to animals. That would put a kink in things anyway," said George "You are going to a lot of expense with this, I hope it produces something."

"I hate it when guys like that run rough shod over things. Racing can be a lot of fun, but he's ruining it for everyone. At least it appears so, I don't mean to convict him without knowing, but I think he's a menace to the whole racing scene," I said. "I can also afford to be nosy and indulge my will. Let's listen to the radio for a bit. The late news is on soon. I like to keep abreast of what is happening in the world."

Mary arrived Tuesday as we were finishing breakfast. George asked her grandfather to stay for a cup of coffee. I showed Mary around as Robert and George welcomed Paul Keifer, Mary's grandfather. We toured the rooms so she knew where to find the laundry hampers. I told her we wanted her to do one at a time so that way the laundry would not get mixed up. I showed her were we kept the vacuum and other tools in our little storage room. I asked her for this week to do the laundry today, and she could do the vacuuming, dusting, sweeping and so forth, on Thursday. As far as the dishes were concerned I asked that she do them both days. Next Tuesday we could see how things were going and discuss anything further. I left her to make a start on the laundry and returned to the kitchen.

A lively discussion was occurring about the best flies to catch trout. Paul Keifer was an ardent fisherman. We had extra poles so we asked him if he'd like to go out with us for the morning fishing. The day had turned out beautiful for fishing, slightly overcast with no hint of rain. He accepted. Robert and I took the canoe, with George and Paul in the runabout. We got them to tow us to one of the bass beds, and they motored off to another. We returned at noon. Paul and George had three, two caught by Paul, one by George. We only had one. The fish stock was piling up. We all sat down for some lunch including Mary, she had proved to be a bit of a whirlwind. She had two sets of laundry done already, and had swept part of the cottage. This looked more and more like a good idea.

John called with an update on the racing scene. Dave had seen the grooms from the McKenzie stable mixing up stuff to give to their horses but had no idea what it might be. He had watched several races that their horses were involved in, a couple of their runners had won and several had lost but the grooms always seemed to have bet on the right horse in the race even if their horse had been a loser. A start at least, even if mostly negative.

"Next time bring your bathing suit and have a swim," I said to Mary. "No need to rush with the job. I'll talk to my neighbor this afternoon to see if they would like you to come to them for cleaning as well. Your grandfather here nearly skunked the rest of us fishing, so you inherit the day's catch. I'll pay you for the day, but you and your grandfather can stay for a while or head home whenever you feel the urge. No need for more work today."

They thanked us and stayed to chat for a while. We told them of Sam's murder and the other things on our collective minds. They told us they had read of the murder and were horrified. We told them of the Penners and the burglaries with all the violence accompanying them as well as alibis and the theories we had. When it came to the horse racing problem, they knew nothing about horse racing but could see the point about cruelty to animals.

"I agree with your assessment of the burglar and the murder," said Paul. "He sounds like a violent man, and it sounds like he was surprised by Sam and killed him."

"That's our theory as well," said George. "Nothing else seems to fit."

Thursday Paul offered to take us to a favorite trout stream of his. George and Robert accepted but I had a bit of business in town and wanted to invite the neighbors for the barbecue on Saturday so I said I would come another time. They grabbed their equipment and away they drove. I visited all the neighbors around our end of the lake, to invite them to the barbecue. Everyone was quite enthusiastic. They liked the idea of a neighborhood get together. Most said they would come and so that gave me some idea of numbers and was pleased at the amount of participation shown. I put my order in for the groceries and drinks needed for the barbecue.

Mary was sitting in the living room crying when I walked back into the cottage. She hadn't heard me arrive. She felt embarrassed and didn't want to tell me about it. I had to put on my best school teacher and mentor, type of face. It turned out that both she and her boyfriend were being bullied by a fellow by the name of Ray Cavanagh. Apparently this fellow was area bully number one. His whole family were suspected of living just outside the law. He always had money, but his was a poor family and he didn't work. He had dropped out of school in grade nine. Nothing had been brought forward to date of a criminal nature, to prove anything was amiss. He considered himself irresistible and was pressuring her hard to have sex with him. Cavanagh had threatened Mary's

boyfriend Ken Nicholson when he had tried to talk to Cavanagh.
Ken Nicholson's father was a local doctor and Ken wanted to
follow in his footsteps. Ken was not into physical violence and
was frightened as well. She had told her mother, but her mother's
only answer to this was to tell her just to say, no and to stay away
from him. That would not help at all. I knew bullies, from my days
as a teacher. When she was calmed down somewhat, I promised
to see what I could do. I also told her I had talked to my neighbor
about a job for her and would know about that later today. The job
possibility cheered her up immensely.

Lunch eaten, I went to town and after a couple of inquiries
tracked down this Cavanagh to a young fellow hanging out beside
the diner. There were two other tough looking young men with
him. I took these to be his cronies.

I walked up to them and said. "I understand you are Ray
Cavanagh?"

"What if I am," he replied.

"You were pointed out to me, so I have a little message for you.
A friend of mine, Mary Keifer was telling me you are trying to
bully her into having sex with you. She doesn't want to, so I'm here
to ask you to leave her alone."

"You're not related to her so it's none of your business."

"You seem to know the family well, so you know her father was killed in the war."

"So what, I still say it's none of your business."

"Since she has no father to stand up for her, and she's a friend of mine, I'm making it my business, so please leave her alone."

"I'll do what I like any time I like. There is no way you can stop me."

"Possibly not, but I'd just like you to think about this. If you do push her into it, I'll know right away. You can maybe bully her into not saying anything, but I'll know anyway, as soon as it happens. Then I'll be coming to see you."

"What can you do? You're nothing but an old man. I'd beat you into a pulp."

"Perhaps you could beat me to a pulp, no doubt you'd have your friends here hold me. You certainly wouldn't chance getting hurt. I have no intention of coming at you like that. A wise man once said 'violence is the last refuge of the incompetent.' I am not incompetent in that way. You would go to jail. I would see to it."

"It would be just her word against mine. I'm not worried about that."

"Then think about this. Maybe the judge wouldn't see it that way. Do you wish to spend several years in jail? Is satisfying your ego worth that? I will continue to watch you until I can

get something on you, then you will definitely go to jail. I will
personally see to it."

The three of them moved in threateningly. I stood my ground
as calmly as I could thinking to myself 'do not show any fear'.
"You can also go to jail for assault. All of you if you wish. I
certainly will report anything of that sort right away to the police."

"I'll do as I please," he repeated.

"I sincerely hope you are not too stupid to change your mind
about this, because I'm quite serious. While we're talking about
this, you can also leave her boyfriend Ken Nicholson alone. Any
rough stuff there and I go to the police as well."

"Get lost I'm tired of listening to you old man," he growled.

"I hope you think about what you would be giving up if you do
anything foolish," I said in parting.

On the way home I stopped off at my neighbor's, the
Hutchinson's to inquire if they had talked about employing Mary.
They had discussed it and they felt it was a good idea. They wanted
to meet Mary. I went to my cottage, got Mary and returned to let
them talk with her. Mary was excited. They liked her right away
and booked her to work for them on Mondays and Wednesdays.
Her weeks were filling up. I told her about my talk with Ray
Cavanagh. I asked her to keep me informed about anything
that happened in that direction, no matter what it might be. She

promised she would. I asked her if she could come out this Friday to make hamburgers for the barbecue Saturday. Another day's pay fit in well for her.

All was ready for her arrival on Friday. I had raw hamburger, to be fixed up for hamburgers and the other needed ingredients. I had purchased lots of pop particularly coke, seven up, ginger ale, and orange crush. Pretzels, potato chips, and other snacks, joined the list. We would be ready for the crowd. I recruited chairs from the same neighbors, to be brought on Saturday.

Mrs. MacGregor called Friday evening, she was very upset. She had a nightmare the previous night that indicated I was going to get badly hurt. I assured her we were being careful and everything was going smoothly. It took a lot to get her calmed down. I told her about the BBQ we were to have and assured her that there was to be many people around.

The Keifer's were invited, not as help but as guests. I had also called my Peterborough friends and invited them. John would bring Will. Jim and Moishe would drive up together. Moishe was even closing the shop for a holiday.

The barbecue day started off beautiful, sun shining, and birds singing, warm but not hot. The lake was ruffled only by a slight breeze. The guests started to arrive at about noon. First the Peterborough contingents, then the town guests and finally the guests from around the lake. By 2:00 P.M. the party was in full swing. People swimming, and others just sitting in the shade chatting. The lemonade, punch and soft drinks were flowing like a river. Everyone in a good mood. Paul Keifer was regaling a big crowd with fish stories, while John and Will were talking horses with whoever would listen, and this included a large crowd of assorted types.

The barbecue was fired up and I began to cook for the crowd. Mary and her mother insisted on helping as did various other ladies. The hamburgers and hot dogs started flowing to the hungry. We showed everyone George's fish barbecue tool. The people trying out the barbecued fish swore it was the best cooked fish they had ever tasted. We had a lot of fish that we had frozen and were hard pressed to keep up with the demand. Some of the ladies had brought pies and other desserts. A bonfire was started in the pit and marshmallows were toasted. A good many were more like burnt offerings, but everyone was having a good time. John and Will brought out their guitar and fiddles. A good old sing song got underway with dancing and much goodwill. Conversations were going all over with many varied topics. Jim, Moishe, George and Robert were in a discussion of Sam's murder. Nothing new was being added but their anger was very apparent. We asked Jim and Moishe to join our patrols, they accepted eagerly. They wanted to do something to contribute. Moishe was extremely pleased to do something toward finding his friend's murderer.

The party went late and we had fireworks which the kids of all ages loved. The kids started falling asleep wherever sleep overtook them. The adults eventually were too exhausted to dance anymore. It had been a good successful party.

Chapter 10

We went back to our old routine to start the week. All three of us were overtired from the busy weekend we had. Fishing and swimming took up most of our time. There was a driving range on our side of town, not too far away, so Monday we hit a bucket of balls each. We still had some major problems but overall seemed to be hitting the ball better than we had been a month ago. We took ourselves to the golf course on Tuesday while Mary cleaned. We each had an exceptionally good round, even dipping into the high eighties. But we consoled ourselves that the course was shorter and easier than we were used to.

Wednesday, Robert and George went fishing in the morning, I headed to town to do the shopping. We were out of everything. I got back late morning. The last thing I remember was walking through the door carrying an armload of groceries. I woke up several minutes later, completely disoriented. I had a very sore head. I was laying down on my stomach. No, I discovered I was tied down. Not only that but my mouth was taped shut, as were my eyes.

"Wakey, wakey," a voice said.

I didn't know the voice. What was going on?

"We're now going to teach you to mind your own business," continued the voice. "You're much too nosy for your own good."

I realized I was stripped to the waist, with my trousers down around my knees. All of a sudden there was pain like I'd never felt before all over my back. I could hardly breathe. The pain was extremely intense, and not confined to one spot. The pain screamed through my senses. My head shot back and I tried to yell. I couldn't yell, my mouth was taped shut. Sweat broke out all over. I felt like throwing up and couldn't because of the tape.

I started to pray in my thoughts, I said 'Dear God if this is what Jesus felt, help me I pray, give me the strength to endure.'

"That was a cat o' nine tails," the voice continued. "A little taste. You'll be feeling more of the same. You have to learn that you should keep to yourself, and not bother your betters. Perhaps we should add a little salt to the mix."

I heard someone else move. Something sprinkled on my back, then the fire broke out even more intense. I sucked in my breath as best I could and endured. I prayed. The fire abated a little but then the whip was applied again. I passed out. I woke. My soul seemed on fire. My whole back down to my knees was nothing but searing pain. Two lashes of the cat later and I passed out for a second time. I could only breathe deep and endure.

"Now then," said the voice calmly. "Am I getting through to you? If I'm not we can keep this up for a while. Here is little more salt to help you think."

"Hey," I heard another voice say. "There's a boat pulling up to the dock, with two guys in it. Let's get out of here."

Salt hit the wounds, I heard a scramble of feet as I passed out again. I woke to hear George say, "God in heaven what has been going on here?"

Robert removed the tape from my mouth and eyes while George untied me. Pain washed over me. I passed out again.

When I came to, I mumbled "Wash!"

"What did you say?" Said George.

"My back." I said weakly breathing through my nose to hold myself together. "Wash the salt off my back, hurry please." Robert had already called the police and asked for an ambulance. George started to wash my back. I passed out. Apparently he quit when I passed out. He told me when I woke. I told him to keep going till the washing was done, and not to worry if I passed out. It had to be done. George was tougher than Robert, he finished the job. When I next woke my back was covered by something cool. The police had arrived and had started to question Robert and George. There wasn't much they could tell them. The something cool on my back turned out to be a soaking wet towel. It felt good.

They tried to question me. I couldn't reply. I could hardly think. I kept drifting in and out of consciousness. George asked them to wait until later. I learned after that one of the neighbors had seen a pickup truck speeding away. Neither George nor Robert had seen it as it was hidden from the dock by the cottage. The neighbor had not taken the license number or paid much attention, other than to say he saw a vehicle.

The ambulance arrived and I was given a shot of something. I went to sleep again this time in more of a normal manner. I woke lying on my stomach in a clinic bed in town... The pain was there, but much muted. A nurse came in and offered me a drink, which turned out to be orange juice in a glass with a straw. I lay there thinking a long time. Eventually a doctor arrived for an examination. His pronunciation was that I would live, but be very sore for a few days. He told me they were going to take me to Ross Memorial hospital in Lindsay, but I asked if it would be okay for me to go to Peterborough as that was our home. I knew it was a bit farther, but not a great deal. He agreed. He mentioned putting in a lot of stitches. That I had already figured out for myself. I said a thank you prayer, to God for not letting them do more damage. The ambulance arrived and the doctor gave me a shot of morphine for the trip. With me out cold we reached Peterborough with little fuss, none on my part.

Thursday dawned to a lot of muted pain. I was offered food, but didn't feel like eating. A detective inspector, a man by the name of Jamieson, came in after the nurse left. He opened by saying," You have some nasty enemies. Any ideas on who they were? I understand you were blindfolded."

"A few ideas," I replied. "Nothing certain. I didn't see them. The voice was one I did not know."

"How many people were there?"

"Three, I think."

"Were any names mentioned?"

"None that I heard."

"How did they get in?"

"The cottage was open, I remember entering, then nothing after that. At least nothing until I came to the first time."

"Do you know what he used to hit you with?"

"I don't know what knocked me out, but what he hit me on the back with, he said was a cat o' nine tails. Plus some salt that they rubbed in between hits."

"The salt was from your own kitchen we think. They must have worn gloves as we found no unusual prints. What were those ideas you mentioned?"

"I think they were people we were looking for in Peterborough, in regard to some burglaries. The burglaries are quite often accompanied by violence. We have been doing patrols, Robert, George and myself. I think it's related to our friend's murder. The police have been getting nowhere. We've been trying to help. If they are the people we think they are I got off lucky, our friend Sam's mouth and nose were taped like my mouth. He suffocated. Maybe they learned a bit from that."

"Why would they think to come after you?"

"I was interviewed just after we volunteered to do the patrols to help. The Peterborough newspaper got hold of the information and interviewed me. How they knew where I was, at my cottage, I mean, I have no idea."

"Okay, you must have got close somewhere."

"About two weeks ago George spotted something suspicious, but couldn't nail it down. Just a truck moving away fast when he got near."

"You said ideas, plural. What else did you think of?"

"On a more local note, I did think it might be a young fellow by the name of Ray Cavanagh. He is a violent person and I had warned him away from my cleaning girl, who he had been harassing."

"Why you?"

"Do you mean why did I talk to him?"

"Yes, doesn't she have her own family to turn to?

"Her father died in the war, her mother felt that just telling Mary to stay away from him was enough. I used to be a school teacher and I know that staying away is never enough. Does that answer your question?"

"Yes it does, the local OPP have had other dealings with that young man. He's a bad apple that's for sure. Why did you mention him second?"

"It wasn't his voice I heard, and I'm almost certain I would have recognized it if it were, but you could check to see if he has an alibi. The other possibility is some people we are looking into in the racing industry, although how they could be linked in here is almost impossible to understand."

"Why are you 'looking into' those racing people?"

"They seem to be involved in fixing races and maybe linked to one of my horses getting sick."

"You should leave such things to the authorities," he said.

At this point a nurse entered and shooed the policeman out, saying I was tired and needed rest. She gave me two tablets with a glass of water and departed. I went to sleep.

A few hours later after I woke up George and Robert were allowed in for a few minutes. "How are you feeling?" ventured Robert.

"As good as I can expect," I replied. "Generally very sore, thanks for being there for me. I also want to say thank you for washing off that salt."

"That was diabolical," said George. "I didn't want to hurt more but I could see your point. You were passed out for most of it and it was just as well that you were."

"The doctor says it was quite clean, so I guess you did a good job."

"How long will you be in here," asked Robert.

"As little as possible," I replied "but at least a week. I wouldn't even contemplate moving yet, it still hurts too much."

"We must have been close that night I scared them off on patrol," said George.

"That's one possibility," I replied "but we mustn't forget that young lad there in Bobcaygeon, young Ray Cavanagh."

"You are definitely right about that, as usual," said George. "I had forgotten about him."

"Maybe you guys can keep an eye on him for a while," I said. "I certainly can't and I think he needs watching."

"We don't want to tire you, but we brought you some grapes. We'll be back every chance we get to keep you up to date with things," said Robert.

They said their goodbyes and left. A short time later pastor Alton and his wife came in for a short visit. I told them that I would be at church on Sunday, a week and a half away, if at all possible. They told me not to rush things too much, but I had always healed quickly and that should be plenty of time.

My sons' with their families were the next in. I was able to reassure them that while my back was a mess at the present time. I would be as good as new in about two weeks three at the most. They were relieved, worried, and full of advice. Ah well, such is life. I realized that they loved me and meant well.

The nurse came in as soon as I was alone and wanted to know if I felt hungry.

"I think I could eat but it's going to be very awkward," I said. "I don't think I could sit up.

"No, you mustn't sit up," she said. "I'll be here to help. Maybe in a couple of days we can let you feed yourself, but for now it'll be one of us." The meal was good, consisting of chicken broth, ice cream and milk.

George and Robert had taken it upon themselves to go to the cottage and ask around there and in Bobcaygeon to see if they could come up with anything to show where the attack had come from. Ray Cavanagh had an alibi as we had thought. Nobody had noticed anything unusual.

I swung between bouts of pain and drug induced sleep for the next day. Pastor and Mrs Alton, came in often. The second day wasn't quite as bad.

George arrived for a visit with Robert. They had no new news.

Robert said, "What do you think our next move should be?"

"The best thing, I would say is to talk to the Peterborough police. What do you think George, you're the ex-cop?" I said.

"That's exactly what we should do," George replied. "We can't leave you here alone so one of us will go and talk to them."

"Hold it, what do you mean you can't leave me alone?" I asked.

"What if they come when we're not around to help? They could finish what we interrupted you know," said George. "In my opinion they weren't finished and he's bad news."

"I suppose it's possible, but I'm here in the hospital just now so I'm relatively safe. Go now and let them know, then we'll discuss further arraignments when you get back," I said.

After a lot of further discussion which got us nowhere, they left for the races and a Saturday night patrol.

Dorset Lightning seemed totally recovered from his bout of diarrhea so he and Sim's Delight were to race Saturday. Both were in races with a good chance to win. Dorset Lightening came in second and Sim's Delight won. Not being able to go to the races to see my horses run was one of life's little annoyances, but overall very good results with good payouts.

John came to visit, they were progressing well with his new barn. He told me Jim had lent him the money for expansion, by a mortgage on the farm. Dave had called and reported that the McKenzie people could get one or two of their horses to break stride almost to order and there didn't appear to be anything that they were doing to make it happen. If they wished to have their horse lose in a lower race so that the odds would be higher next time. It always broke.

Our patrols showed nothing.

Robert and George went to bed, and then to church followed by the trip back to the lake. The church bulletin had been written by the pastor's wife. The church secretary was away for a couple of weeks. No fun at all. No mistakes.

The new film version of 'The King and I', had debuted in the theaters and we talked about going to see it. It was starring Deborah Kerr and Yul Brynner, critics were saying it would probably be film of the year.

Mrs Wilson, Mrs Johnson and Mrs. MacGregor came in a group together. All three quite distressed, but a bit relieved to find I was in good spirits. They were quite upset about the extent of my injuries and were angry that the people who had done this had not only not been apprehended but totally unknown.

They had just left when the Keifer family came to visit. They had traveled down to Peterborough in the old car, to see how I was doing. When they came in it gave me an idea, so after the greetings I said, "I just had a thought. I'm going to be laid up for a bit and won't be able to do any yard work around the cottage. I wonder Paul do you feel up to a few chores, I would pay you of course?"

"You don't need to pay me, it would be a privilege," said Paul "What sort of chores were you thinking about?"

"We can discuss them later, perhaps you could come back after the ladies leave or stay later?" I said. "We don't need to bore them with the details. Thank you all for coming to see me, I get bored laying here." It took a while but, we eventually exhausted the news of the happenings around the village, cottage and the Keifer family. I thanked them for coming and on leaving Paul suggested this evening he could come back for a talk

Paul arrived with visiting hours, and with a box of chocolates. I thanked him for the chocolates, everybody likes chocolates.

"You seemed to have more on your mind than what you said," was Paul's opening line. "That's why I didn't question you further in front of the girls."

"Well, yes, good of you to notice," I replied. "I'm worried about Mary as well as the yard work." I told him about my talk with the Cavanagh boy. He was not totally unaware of the situation.

"I don't need to be paid however it would be a privilege."

"Don't worry, I can afford it. I need you for that, and I think he might try something as soon as he hears that I'm a bit laid up. He's not very bright and he might think it's time to make his move. He might think if Mary is alone out at the cottage and that it's a perfect time. I do need the yard work done out there and having you there kills two birds with one stone, so to speak. You look pretty fit, but I don't want to put a physical strain on you. The work need not be strenuous. You could weed the flower beds, and generally keep everything tidy."

"You have one of those new gas driven lawn mowers do you not?"

"Yes, but it still needs to be pushed, that's not always easy. I don't want you having a heart attack over a stupid lawn."

"If you're worried, I could do a little at a time."

"I'll tell Mary to keep an eye on you," We both chuckled.

"I have been wanting something to do, I'm pretty fit, and I feel useless. Joan struggles to make ends meet and I only have the pension. We do all right but things are tight."

"Okay, then it's settled. You do the yard work, don't go at it too hard. It's just a cottage. I like it to look nice, but you would be a godsend to me. You are totally in charge, if you see something needs to be done, go ahead and do it. If it looks too big for you then come to me please with a suggestion and we'll discuss it."

We shook hands on the deal. When he left I felt much better in my soul. I lay awake for a long while thinking about the situation. Eventually the nurse came and gave me a shot to help me sleep.

Chapter 11

Since I was incapacitated, George and Robert decided to take a day and look into the reports issuing from Dave, in Toronto, about the McKenzie horses.

The Toronto racing meet was in full summer mode, racing almost every day. Robert and George went to Toronto to have a look at the things, as reported by Dave. They couldn't get into the barns, but Dave showed them one of the horses that was doing the breaking. He was entered in that night's racing. True to form as he was leading he broke and lost. Dave pointed out the grooms. They were laughing, an unusual reaction for a stable that had just lost a race. The stable won another race that night with their horse enjoying long odds, stranger and stranger. Yet try as they did, they found nothing they could lay their finger on. There was maybe some hanky panky going on, but it was well hidden. George's detective nose was aquiver. He told Dave once again to stay away, just keep an eye on things from a distance and keep reporting. Dave promised he would keep his distance.

George and Robert came back to Peterborough. George went to John's farm to talk to the Jones fellow to see if he could shed some light on the things Dave had noticed.

"Did you ever notice anything about a horse breaking, or them teaching a horse somehow to break?" George asked.

"I was never allowed to go to the races," said Jones, "but I did overhear a conversation once that made me wonder. I never saw them training a horse that way, but they were laughing one time and the head groom took something out of his pocket and did something and one of the horses started jumping around for a minute. I didn't hear or see anything to make him do that."

"You said he took something from his pocket, but you didn't see what it was, it must have been small. How big would you say it was?"

"I would say it wasn't more than 2 or 3 inches long, by about 2 inches at most in width or thickness. He hid it in one hand easily. He held it to his face so he could have had a whistle or something like that, but I heard nothing."

"Did they have another location where they kept horses?"

"I think there was another place, but it wasn't around the farm. They would take a horse away for a couple of weeks and when they came back, his legs were kept bandaged and he would shy from them for a while."

"Do you think they were using some kind of torture to train the horse to be afraid?"

"I don't know, but they sure were a cruel bunch."

George's nose was quivering even worse, but he couldn't think of anything else to ask, so he came to the hospital to talk to me.

"How are you feeling today?" George asked when he was settled in.

"Not so sore today, a couple of more days and I'll be ready to head home. How are things on the investigation fronts?"

"Robert and I were in Toronto yesterday, McKenzie's horses break when they need to lose and win at long odds when you least expect it. They seem to know though and have bets were they will do the most good. I guess that's not new news."

"Were you watching the driver when the horse broke?"

"That's just it the driver seemed to be totally unaware of the situation. Dave says they don't always use the same driver, but it seems to be a catch driver that it happens to, not one of their own. Which makes it really hard to say that they are up to anything."

"Are you saying that it's their driver on the winning drives?"

"That's the case. There always seems to be another horse not necessarily trained by them that does measure up to what you would think by looking at the program and is usually the favorite but just doesn't seem to have much zip. To top it off McKenzie's stable and driver seem to know it's going to happen. It's frustrating!"

"They must be doing something, but what?" I said

"I thought so as well, so I went and had a talk to that Jones fellow. He didn't add much to what we knew, he said again that they were a cruel bunch and occasionally they would take a horse elsewhere for a few days or a week and then the horse would return, very skittish and with bandages on his legs. I asked him about torture, but he knew nothing of that sort. I asked him about other locations that they might have and he confirmed that there was such a place, he didn't know where. It occurred to me that they may be using a dog whistle. Humans wouldn't hear it but dogs do, maybe horses as well."

"I guess the best we can say at the present, is that there is something afoot, but we're as far away from knowing what as we were at the start. The problem must exist at the track here as well, I just don't want it hitting out at us. Maybe it already has though," I said.

"I think we need to rethink our strategy. Do you think if Robert and I drove back out to Norwood, that we might be able to track down that fellow we talked to before? The big question is would he know for instance where this extra property might be located and so on. Do you think that might be a logical next step?"

"Well, it would help if we knew, we might then be able to keep it under some kind of surveillance. We do have a lot of other stuff on our plate though."

149

"We would have to forego some of the fishing trips to the cottage for sure, but when we're here we could do some surveillance if we knew where to look," said George. "Robert and I will go out to Norwood tomorrow and see what we can come up with. When will you be able to get out of here?"

"I might be up to it day after tomorrow, the pain is not as severe as it was, and I'm tired of lying here. Tired of the food as well. I'll see if I can sit up a little later today. I'll still have to lay down mostly for a while."

"OK let's go with that for now, I'll leave now and go see Robert about tomorrow, but before I go, a little humor to help you sleep."

"This lady goes into a sporting goods store to get fishing gear for her grandson's birthday. She sees a package deal, so she takes it to the clerk. The clerk has dark glasses on and tells her he's blind but if she drops it on the table he'll know what it is.

'That's a six-foot Shakespeare rod with a Zebco 300 reel and 10-LB. test line. It's a good all-around combination and it's on sale this week for only $20.00.'

She's amazed and as she reaches for her purse, she lets out a sharp "toot". She'd had some beans for breakfast. She's embarrassed, but decides to say nothing, knowing he's blind and won't know it was her.

She turns back to the counter and the clerk gives her a bill for $34.50. She protests to the clerk that he had said it was $20.00. That's true says the clerk, but it's an extra $10.00 for the duck call and $4.50 for the bear repellant.

I hurt all over as I laughed.

Later that evening I tried sitting up for a while. It was now a week and more since I got hurt. As long as I was on a nice soft cushion, it was bearable for a short period. A small step, but a definite one. The pastor and wife came to visit and found me sitting. While they were there, I didn't notice much pain, but I was glad to lay down again when they left. I had overdone things. That night I broke out in a bad fever and was weak as a kitten. The doctor was not amused.

The same waitress was in the Norwood diner when George and Robert arrived. They asked her if she remembered them and it turned out that she did, so they asked her about the man they had been talking to the last time they were there. She said he came in usually every day for a coffee, but she hadn't seen him today. The man in question walked in for his morning coffee just then, so George asked him to sit with them and bought him his coffee.

"Last time we were here a couple of weeks ago we were talking about the McKenzie farm. Do you remember the conversation?" said George.

"Yes quite well," he replied.

"We're kind of looking into things in an unofficial way," said George, "Do you mind talking to us about it?"

"No not at all," he replied, "but I don't know much about the operation, and nothing at all about horse racing."

"We understand he has another location beside the farm buildings where he trains the horses, do you know where that is?"

"I don't know, but maybe you mean that old barn a couple of concession roads from the back of the property, there is a little barn and a bit of a track up off the second line north. It's set back into the woods a little but they may use it once in a while. I don't think anyone owns the property now. The old guy that used to farm there had a couple of race horses and was friendly with McKenzie."

"That must be what we're looking for, can you tell us how to find the place?"

"Yes, but I wouldn't go around there, as I said they are not very welcoming about anyone seeing what they're doing, one of my friends got a rude reception when he was parked near there to do a little partridge hunting."

"We'll be careful, but we need to know how to get there," said George.

He gave us directions and we chatted a while about the weather and other things, then we took our leave and went around to the line which he told us about, running to the north of the farm. We found the place without a lot of trouble. It was tucked back in the woods as he had said. There didn't seem to be anything going on at the moment.

"It does look like an ideal place for partridge," observed Robert, "maybe we could use that as a camouflage for looking around. I wouldn't mind getting a couple of partridge for our efforts."

"That sounds like a top notch idea to me," said George. "I think that should be the next step. We could get our guns and come back later. Perhaps we should park a way down the road to have a good excuse and wander around until we get close to the barn, but be real cautious."

They couldn't do much more right now so they decided to go back to Peterborough. We had made another small step forward. We would come back better prepared to do a little snooping next time.

George and Robert had expected to pick me up the next day, I was in bad shape, and the doctor said at least a week. They had snuck in to visit.

"It looks as though they do some training in this rear facility or whatever you might call it. I think we should try to do a little surveillance on it to see if we can learn anything. Robert suggested we could cover it by doing a little partridge hunting at the same time. It seems to me it would be a good camouflage and we would be armed as well so the horse trainers wouldn't be likely to get too aggressive," said George.

"I agree," I replied, "today is Friday. I'm stuck in here but, you could do some watching of that rear McKenzie property next week. Who knows what you might see."

"George and I will do the patrols tomorrow after the races. We'll take Jim and Moishe, so we'll be two in a car for the night, then maybe George and I can do a little watching at the farm Monday and Tuesday," said Robert. "We may get a partridge or two as well. Partridge make good eating. We might as well get a little recreation out of this." The nurse with doctor in tow arrived at this point and shooed them out. They were told maybe a visit could happen tomorrow but not today.

On Saturday's patrol, about 2:00 A.M. Robert and Jim came upon a house all in darkness with a pickup truck alongside in the driveway. The truck was idling. Robert got out of the car to investigate. He started up the driveway only to hear someone say, "I told you to mind your own business, don't you ever learn?" He was hit immediately with a club which knocked him down as the hit was hard and violent. The thugs closed in and started to hit him with the club and kick him. Jim seeing what was happening honked the horn and moved in with the car. The thugs got into the idling pick up and sped away up the street. Jim didn't pursue but went to Robert who was laying on the ground moaning. Jim got him in the car and drove straight to the hospital. Luckily nothing was broken, but very bad bruising. When he could, Jim radioed George and Moishe and told them what had happened. They all went to the hospital while Robert was treated. He was told to take it easy for a couple of days. The biggest problem was he was extremely angry. Nothing was going to stop him going on the partridge hunting expedition.

When they arrived Sunday we got down right away to discuss strategy.

"I know we've been getting hurt lately, but I think we're finally getting somewhere on both fronts," said George "It's obvious from the comment to Robert that your beating and his are linked. If you guys want to back off, then I understand, but if we carry on we need to be more careful. On the McKenzie front, I don't think they know we exist at the moment, but we still need to be careful. How do you fellows feel about it?"

"As for me," said Robert, "They have made me feel very angry and ridiculous. I want to push harder than before, but I agree, we need to take better care not to be caught out like that again. My vote goes to continue."

"Mine too," I added

George said, "If you, who have been hurt the worst, vote to continue, I feel I can continue as well."

"I can't desert my friend Sam now," said Moishe. "I think we're getting close as well."

"That makes it unanimous," said George, I'm glad to hear that. We can be more cautious, we've been a bit careless and they're taking advantage. We can act the innocent out hunting behind McKenzie's farm. At least this time, and as I said we will have our shotguns. Let's then give Monday a pass and that will give Robert a chance to heal then we'll head out to see if we can get a brace of partridge.

With Robert on the limp Monday they just sat on the veranda all day, drinking coffee with George supplying the odd dumb joke. Tuesday Robert declared himself fit for the hunt. George and Robert set out so they would be at the site around 10:00 A.M. They parked about half a mile down the road and started by making a sweep for partridge down the opposite side of the road. They were in luck and quickly had two. Bagged by Robert who had a good eye for that sort of thing. They had passed the barn, and since there didn't appear to be anyone around they crossed the road and worked their way toward the barn. When they got close George hollered "Hello the barn, is anyone there." There was no answer so they proceeded closer, keeping a close watch for anything. The barn had a bit of a track running around it. As they got close they heard a sound from within.

"I think there's a horse in there," said George.

They approached cautiously and tried the door. It opened readily. There was indeed a horse in the barn, and on closer inspection, they could see that the horse was in pain and had bad looking wounds on its shins. They quickly looked around, and then got out of there, in case someone would come by, to see about the horse. They skirted around the edge of an open field so they were eventually in the woods on the far side of the farm, with the barn and track in sight but about half a mile away.

"You know," said George, "this may be a good place to keep watch on that place. We'd have to use fairly powerful binoculars, but there's a good view from here, as well as decent cover."

"I agree, "said Robert, "we could keep the shotguns as well and that would still give us an excuse in case they saw us."

"They are obviously hurting the horse somehow, but I was thinking that maybe they could be using a dog whistle and blowing it while hurting the horse, then later if they just blew the whistle, the horse would expect to be hurt and would jump or break stride. That would do it."

"Yes that sounds right, but how could we confirm that?"

"Perhaps we could get one of those whistles. I don't know anyone that has a dog that we could test it out with, but if we could, then we could bring the dog here and see if it reacts in any way."

"That's a good thought," said Robert, "meanwhile let's stay here for a while and see if anyone shows up."

"Okay with me." replied George. "I think they may be using an electrical charge to hurt the horse, did you see the electrical high voltage gear in there?"

"Yes, I noticed. I think that's exactly what they're doing."

They waited 2 hours, but that was the last of their luck for the day. It had been a good day, they were hungry so they gave up and went home. I was waiting patiently to hear the report. George and Robert took turns telling of the trip to get some partridge and observe the lie of the land around the back end of the McKenzie property when they visited later that day. What they had found more or less confirmed the suspicions we already had concerning that farm. They had not observed anything definite, so we would have to try again. They would go again Wednesday and Thursday

provided they saw no activity, but couldn't keep it up in case they

in turn were seen. We still didn't want them figuring out that

we were suspicious of them. George took the partridge to Mrs.

MacGregor who latched onto them as if they were gold. She said

she loved preparing them and when George offered to clean them

she pretended she was quite affronted. She declared that no man

knew how to clean them properly. She announced they would be

tonight's supper and invited George and Robert to come for dinner.

Chapter 12

After seeing nothing all day Wednesday at McKenzie's farm they came and asked me if they could go fishing at the cottage for a couple of days, they were very wound up and needed to relax to get things in perspective. They felt if they could get away for a couple of days they could maybe do some thinking. I agreed and gave them the keys. I felt very jealous.

The time for me was passing very slowly. The pastor and wife came to visit as did Mrs.' Wilson and Johnston, still the week dragged slowly by. Mrs. MacGregor came but declared me a malingerer and told me to brace up and get out of there. She was never one to coddle anyone. I guess she felt embarrassed, I missed her too.

Finally the weekend arrived and so did Robert and George. I could see George was excited when he arrived on Saturday. "What has you excited," I asked

"We may have hit a bit of a break through," said George, settling into the one easy chair. Robert took the hard backed one. "We drove back up to the cottage and talked to several people in town about that Cavanagh kid. It looks like he has a cast iron alibi, but he has an older brother, who seems to me quite interesting. The older brother was quite a bad one around there, before the war. He went off to war, much to the relief of the surrounding community. He was a sniper in the war, a very good one apparently, but he lost his stripes several times for cruel "jokes" but was let off because nobody died nor was badly hurt, and they needed his rifle to kill Nazis. Anyway when he returned after the war he began his old habits, until the law got after him big time. He moved away, they think to Peterborough. His name is James Cavanagh, everyone calls him Jimmy."

"Do you think he's our burglar, perhaps even our murderer," I asked. I felt excited that we had at last a name for a suspect.

"For my money he seems to be the guy," said George emphatically.

"I agree," concurred Robert. "There is a Bobcaygeon connection at least. What is our next step?"

"The best thing, I would say is to talk to the Peterborough police. What do you think George, you're the ex-cop?" I said.

"That's exactly what we should do," George replied. "We now know where that comment to Robert came from when they caught him the other night."

"Yes indeed, that would certainly account for the remark. Maybe they thought it was me, they might not know they hurt me this much," I replied.

"What if they come here when we're not around to help you. They could finish what we interrupted you know," said George. "In my opinion they weren't finished and he's bad news."

"I think that's being overly cautious. I suppose it's possible, but I'm here in the hospital just now so I'm relatively safe. Go now and let the police know, then we'll discuss further arrangements when you get back," I said.

They left to talk to the police promising to come back and let me know how it went. They arrived back for the late evening visiting hours. They would then have a couple of hours sleep before doing the patrol areas for the night.

"We talked to the Peterborough police, and they had never heard of the fellow. They were however, quite pleased to have a name to follow up," were George's opening remarks. "They are going to check with the OPP as well to see if they have anything on the guy."

"We haven't involved the Ontario Provincial Police before," said Robert, "but it might be time we expanded things a little. I presume we're not giving up on our efforts?"

Definitely not," I said "We can't let this bunch bully us. I'll heal and I've never given up on anything in my life before. Now is not the time to start. I do think we should be careful. I mean use the radio transmitters more and make sure if we see something, we call each other in as back up. I'll be out of things for maybe two weeks, but I'd like to see you guys keep up the patrols. Paul is going to help as he can keep me, as well as Mary, company over the times you guys are in Peterborough on watch. I'll return to the cottage when I'm able, sometime next week. I think I'll be alright there with Paul over the weekends. I'll put the phone next to the bed, get some better locks and keep them locked. After your patrols, maybe you can return to the cottage the next day and we can compare notes."

"That sounds good," said George. "I feel more relaxed with these arrangements, Robert and I have talked about a game of golf on Monday, and maybe you'll feel up to a trip to the cottage on Tuesday or Wednesday. I heard a good one about golf the other day."

"This avid golfer was on the course with his wife one day. He played a shot on the fifth that sliced so badly it ended up in the gardener's equipment shed. Looking in the door, the couple saw the ball sitting right in the middle of the room. "Look," volunteered the golfer's wife, "if I hold the door open, you can play a shot from here to the green.'

This struck the golfer as an interesting challenge, but, alas, the ball missed the open door and struck his wife on the temple, killing her instantly.

Many years later, the widower was playing with a friend when he hit the exact same slice. The two of them walked into the shed, and, sure enough, there sat the ball in the middle of the room. "I tell you what," said the friend "If I hold the door open, I bet you can get the ball back onto the green."

"Oh, no," said the golfer, shaking his head. "I tried that once before and it took me seven shots to get out."

We all had a good laugh. "Don't make me laugh," I pleaded. "It hurts. I know this is contradictory but it's starting to feel better. I even made it to the bathroom myself this morning. I'm quite proud of that. Can't sit down very well yet though."

"Have you any idea what the schedule is for your healing?" Asked Robert.

"I'll take it slow. I can stand up okay and I can lay on my stomach, but anything else is still pretty gruesome. By next week I'll have another week or more of inactivity," I said.

"We'll come back and see you tomorrow afternoon after church and let you know how we did on the patrol," said George.

"That sounds good, I get pretty bored here, but I think Pastor Alton and maybe wife are coming on Sunday afternoon, so I'll be fine."

George and Robert would do the patrols tonight with Moishe and Jim. Tuesday or Wednesday of next week, I should be allowed to go back out to the cottage. I probably wouldn't be very mobile yet, but at least I wouldn't be laying around here and my back was very near healed.

Pastor Alton and wife were my afternoon visitors on Sunday after church and lunch. "How are you feeling today?" were their first words.

"Stiff, sore and kind of grouchy, from being cooped up in here," I replied, "How did the Sunday service go? I would have liked to have been there, but should make next Sunday. I'm getting a lot of people in to see me lately. George and Robert are in and out and Paul was down from the cottage to visit."

"They are very nice people and good to be around. They help in many ways and are always supportive," said Pastor Alton

"I'm sure you're being too kind," I replied.

"My sermon was on the beatitudes, I like that portion of Matthew, and it can be used in so many ways to produce a good sermon."

"Do you mean just the beatitudes or the whole of Jesus' sermon on the mount?"

"Well I mean the whole of the sermon on the mount. Something you could do for us while you're lying here, is to think up some mottoes or sayings for our new bulletin board."

"How about "No God, no peace, know God, know peace," I suggested

"Yes, that's the sort of thing we need," He said excitedly. "Keep at it. Write them down if you think of more and we'll discuss them later."

Robert and George returned in the afternoon, bringing greetings from all my friends. This included good wishes from Mrs Wilson, Mrs. MacGregor and Mrs. Johnson. Everyone was upset at what had happened to me. George and Robert also reported seeing nothing but the police said there was a violent robbery Saturday night. The thieves must have thought the house was empty, but the husband was home, the wife and kids had gone to the mother's parents for the week end. The husband had been badly beaten and was in hospital.

Monday the doctor examined me and proclaimed that I could go home tomorrow as long as I didn't try to get around at all. I was to come back Friday to see about getting the stitches out. I was heartily glad to see the back of the hospital. I knew I should be grateful that it was there. The ambulance was hired to give me a drive back to the cottage as I still had to lay on my stomach. I could walk a little but still had little strength or stamina. George and Robert made a big fuss over my return. A neighbor had heard that I was due back and had come over with a big casserole. It

felt like heaven. The country air was like a stimulant. The day
was bright and clear. The peace and quiet uninterrupted. Mary
had come out to cook for us. It tasted much better than I usually
produced. A very thoughtful family.

Shortly after supper, Paul arrived and went fishing with
George. They vowed to come back with a nice fish feed for
tomorrow's lunch or dinner. Robert and I settled down to a game
of chess. The board was placed on a chair near the bed and Robert
sat on the floor. I had very much missed our usual interchange of
the news of the world over a game of some kind. Robert proved
to be much the better player, I wasn't concentrating very well
with my various aches and pains. The two games we played were
enjoyable in that it kept my mind off my troubles to some extent.
We discussed our efforts to get our burglar friend. I felt frustrated
because I couldn't contribute more than talk at present. Robert was
convinced it was only a matter of time until we spotted them on
one of our patrols. He was sure we had been close several times,
but were just missing a break through.

On the racing scene, John had several winners so far this
summer. Robert brought me up to date. Dorset Lightning had so
far won twice. Kingston Kenny was winning regularly and was
competing in the invitationals and top class. John was pleased that
he was doing so well at the big track in Toronto. Jake Sheldrake's

horses were also winning regularly. John was having a very successful time, and was thinking of setting up a bit of a stud farm operation. My little slow coach of a mare was going to be the first to give birth on the farm in a while, but it looked like she was to be the first of many. I began thinking of buying a top notch horse to put out to stud. I could give John a couple of shares in him, as part of the fees. It would be an encouragement to him and could pay off big time if the progeny turned out any good. I didn't know how many shares there should be, but I knew it depended on how energetic the horse was and on how many mares he could cover without stress in a season.

George and Paul returned after dusk with a big pickerel, about six pounds and a bass. They had already cleaned them ready for the cook the next day. It would have to be Mary they claimed as George and Robert said they couldn't cook anything. We had to hope Mary was willing. Paul thought she would be. Paul said she loved to cook and we never gave her a chance. So she got her chance. The result was superb. As good a meal as I'd had in many a day. Better than most restaurants. She was immensely pleased by the compliments she received. We went for a swim after that magnificent repast, that is Mary, Paul, George and Robert did. I lay on the dock on a towel. The doctor had very particularly told me not to swim or even get in to cool off until he gave the word. It was a great day.

Wednesday was much the same lazing around the cottage on my stomach and watching others swim. We had a nice T-bone steak cooked by George on the barbecue. It seemed he was brave enough to try to barbecue at least. He did a great job. Dinner of baked potatoes and steak was fit for a king. Friday Paul took me into town to the clinic to see about removal of the stitches. The drive into the clinic in Bobcaygeon was painful but endurable. The doctor said they were healing nicely but to give myself until Monday before I moved around a lot, as there were so many. I wasn't pleased but understood his concern. My back was quite itchy, so he gave me some salve for relief and sent me home.

As luck would have it we met Ray Cavanagh as we were leaving the clinic. He had his usual number of hangers on with him.

"Well, well," he sneered, "What have we here? I do believe it's a cripple. You shouldn't stick your nose into other people's business. Serves you right."

"I won't be laid up very long," I replied, "Don't think I've quit watching out for you and your shenanigans. This temporary disability doesn't change anything I said before. I must thank you though for clearing up my mind on a certain question that has been bothering me."

"I don't know what you're talking about." he snarled back.

"That's okay with me I said, just think about what you said for a while," I said "It will come to you." We turned away and proceeded to the car.

"Why did you say thank you to that Cavanagh kid?" asked Paul.

"He leaks information like a sieve," I said, "What he said was I should keep my nose out of other people's business. That's exactly what the fellow that beat me up, said, it makes one think that he may be heard it elsewhere, don't you think?"

"Yes, you're right. I didn't think of that, but it makes perfect sense."

"The trouble is we don't know for sure, he may have just accidentally said it, because of the situation, but on the whole I think he knew. What do you say to a cup of coffee at the diner? I survived the ride in sitting, so I can try for a few moments more, while I think. I just need my cushions."

When we got seated with a coffee I said, "The violent burglar is almost certainly Ray's older brother James. All the evidence points that way, but it's only circumstantial. We have no real proof. The problem still remains, how do we find this James and bring him to justice?"

"There may be a way, James had a girlfriend here before the war, and I think he still comes to see her. While he's here I can see him talking to Jimmy. His girlfriend may know where he is. She's a little on the weak side mentally. She's had at least one child by him and has had another since the war was over. He started by abusing her sexually before the war. That's probably why Ray thinks he can do whatever he wants. She thinks he's great. I could talk to her and see if she knows where he is," said Paul pensively.

"I would advise against it," I said, "Look at what happened to me. If he thought you were pumping her for information, he would blow his stack, anything could happen. It's a good thought though, maybe there is a way without her repeating the questions to him and arousing his suspicion. We can at least think about it and see if we can see a way. We better head home my back is still pretty tender as the doctor said."

Robert and George had been busy staying out of Mary's way. She had again cooked us a nice fish lunch with mashed potatoes and carrots. She certainly knew how to cook. I lay down to give my abused back a chance to heal a little more. The rest went for a swim. I was exhausted and went right to bed to sleep most of the afternoon away. Paul stayed with me and puttered around the

garden while George and Robert golfed. Then George and Paul
went evening fishing while Robert listened to his radio programs
and kept me company. The big news was that the cruise liner
Andrea Doria had sunk after been hit by Swedish Liner Stockholm
in a fog, 45 miles south of Nantucket with loss of life set at 51. Also
Egypt had nationalized the Suez Canal. We weren't sure of the
significance of that last. The liner collision must have been a sheer
fluke, to have a collision like that with all that expanse of ocean.

George caught an eight pound Muskie. John called Friday night
with the news that Dave had been spoken to by the McKenzie
grooms. They had asked him why he was always watching them.
He told them he was new to racing and they had a good barn. He
wanted to learn from the best methods. I asked John to call Dave
and caution him to be careful. I was worried. I woke Saturday
morning to find George and Robert getting ready to go to
Peterborough for their patrol Saturday night.

Chapter 13

I was feeling better, so on Monday I went to John's farm to see about the horses and to ask if he knew a dog that we could test with a dog whistle.

"How is the horse training business going? You seem to have grown quite a bit this summer?" I asked when John came to talk.

"Very well thanks," he replied, "that groom is working out very well. He's a hard worker and understands the work well. I'm glad I let you fellows talk me into hiring him. As you can see the new barn is coming along well."

"I'm glad Jones turned out so well. Do you have him working on the barn as well?"

"Oh yes, he can turn his hand to anything. He's a terrific find. The horses are in fine fettle as well, we should have a good chance for a win or two on the week end. Dave called last night as well, I didn't call because it was late. He reports that one of the McKenzie horses that he trains but doesn't own foundered in the barns. The vet couldn't think how a horse that is kept in a barn and exercised regularly, in other words kept fit and lean could founder. The vet had the feed checked and a lot of other things, but he said he was stumped."

"The technical term for that is laminitis isn't it?"

"Yes, I think that's right," said John, "I'm not a great one for these new terms, I always knew it as founder. I don't think they could give a horse that, I don't know, it's a condition usually brought on by eating feed too high in sugar, I think. I heard that a horse can get it early in the spring or when there's too high a sugar content in the pasture because of frost. I wouldn't put anything past these birds. Seems kind of farfetched though. The thing that bothers me if they did give the horse something, why risk a good horse in that way, it's sometimes deadly? Friday I have Sundown Sheila and my new client's horse going, its name is Georgian Sam and Saturday, Dorset Lightning and Jake's Sim's Delight. They all have a good chance. Will has the job of the driving of them."

"You are definitely having a good summer, and why not, you are a good trainer. It's nice to see you having some good results. This business can be frustrating. By the way I wanted to know if you knew anybody that has a dog that is used to a dog whistle, does anyone around here train dogs that way?"

"As a matter of fact Joe McAllister does that. He uses a couple of dogs to help herd his sheep. He can't whistle with just his mouth, because of loss of teeth. He came here from Scotland after the war and just sort of carried on as he had in the old country."

"Where does he live? I'd like to talk to him."

"What are you up to now?" asked John. "You've always got some weird idea going.

"Oh, it's just a notion."

John gave the directions and I wrote them down. I took my leave without further explanation and headed for Joe McAllister's farm. He was just coming out of the house after his mid-morning snack when I arrived. I saw this grizzled old fellow with two typical English border collies in attendance. His eyes had a smile in them as if he was enjoying the world. I didn't know how to approach the problem, so I just explained what was going on and hoped for the best. When I explained about the horses, the suspicious training, and how we thought that they may be using a dog whistle, he caught on in a flash. He appeared to be the typical canny old Scot.

"What is it that you'll be wanting, young fellow?" he said.

"I don't really know," I replied, "I just thought if we could somehow confirm that they were abusing the horses that way, we could maybe show the authorities and have them put a stop to it."

"I'm with you there," he said, "I like animals, horses 'specially, cruelty really gets my dander up."

"I guess I was hoping I could borrow one of your dogs to try to confirm what goes on, I could bring him back in an hour or two."

"Yes, well I can see what your gettin' at," he said, "I'd like to help, as I said I don't like to see cruelty to animals. My dogs work best for me they're kind of shy around strangers. Let me introduce them. The dog is Ozzie and the bitch is Emma, they like people and are quite friendly, they would appreciate a pat to show them you're friendly. Why don't I go along with you and have a look at this set up, and we can decide how to go about it?"

"They are a dangerous bunch, I don't want to get you into a mess. I just thought that if we could see how the dog reacts as they are doing this so called 'Training' then we would know for certain," I replied while giving the dogs a pat on the back. They responded by much tail wagging and generally showing their approval.

While we were talking he had got a glint in his eye and I realized he kind of felt he would be getting one up on this bunch. He was displaying the love of the Scots to be up to mischief.

"I'd love to help mister but I couldn't let my dogs go without me along, how about it?"

"I'll tell you what, let me talk to my friends and we'll figure out where we go from here. Can I call you tomorrow and discuss it with you?"

"I don't have a phone, but I'm not so far, why not come back out if you want to follow up with this?" he said.

"It's a deal," I replied, "I'll come back out on Monday afternoon and let you know in any case."

After shaking hands on the deal and I drove back to Peterborough. The long weekend was ahead with our BBQ to set up.

Thursday we picked up McAllister with his two dogs and his dog whistle. He had a gleam is his eye, all Scots seemed to love to be subtle and be up to a bit of mischief. We drove to where George and Robert were waiting and then to the place they hid their cars. We got the dogs out, grabbed our shotguns to give us our alibi for being there. We formed a line in the bush on the side of the road opposite the barn. Right away you could see it was good partridge country. McAllister set the dogs out ranging through the bush, and within a few minutes we had two partridge. Our cover established we headed for their blind that they had used to observe the barn. We just arrived when the grooms arrived at the barn in their pick up.

"There they are," said George, "let's wait and see what they're going to do. Yesterday they got the horse out almost immediately. They might even have two horses in there for all we know."

"Do you want me to give the whistle a toot now?" said McAllister.

"Let's wait and see what they do first," said George. "Everybody stay well down and don't move in case they see us too soon. Make sure the dogs stay still as well."

"Aye, they'll mind," said McAllister softly.

The men at the barn went about their business. They got the horse out and harnessed it to the sulky. The horse obviously didn't want anything to do with it, but finally stood trembling between the shafts.

"Now give your whistle a blow," said George.

He gave a long blast. We heard nothing, but there was an immediate reaction. The dogs perked up their ears and the horse gave a scream and started running. The men at the barn weren't ready for that and one got knocked over by the horse. The poor animal had nowhere to go but around the track, but it tried to jump the rails and got hung up. The men got up and slowly recovered the horse. They looked all around, then slowly led the horse back to the barn. While they were inside George suggested it was time to get out of there. We headed back to the cars. We were walking along the road when the pickup from the barn drove up.

"What are you doing wandering around here?" demanded the driver angrily.

"Just hunting some partridge," replied George calmly, holding up the game bag with the birds in it, "what's the trouble?"

"You just stay away from here!" he went on as angry as before, "you're disturbing our animals and we don't like it."

"Who is 'we'," replied George. "This is vacant land, we checked, so we can be here whenever we wish to."

"We own the land over there," said the driver pointing to the other side of the road, "and we have animals there that you are disturbing. So beat it and don't come back."

McAllister started to say something in protest so I gripped his arm hard to keep him silent.

"We don't want to upset you, young fellow," George was saying, "But we have every right to hunt over there if we wish. We don't come here often anyway and we'll try to stay away from your operation, but we can be here if we want to."

"Just stay away from here, or else," he replied.

"That's not very friendly," said George.

"I'm not trying to be friendly, get out of here," He said as they drove away in a spray of gravel.

"I guess we've been warned," said Robert.

"It looks like it," I said "but he must know that we can be here if we wish to, and there is nothing he or anyone else can do about it. That's good partridge country there, it took us less than ten minutes to get that pair we have."

"There's also a nice little creek that runs through the property as well, and it has quite a few ducks in it," said Robert. "Altogether a good hunting property. There's probably deer in there as well."

"I wish you had let me say something to that rude young fellow," said McAllister. "I'd have put a flea in his ear, I'll tell you."

"I bet you could have too," I said. "But it would just have got him madder, and just now we don't wish to get him suspicious of us. Would you like to have the partridges we got for a meal, Mr. McAllister?"

"That's quite decent of you to ask, Mr. Withers, I would love to have them, but I didn't do much to earn them."

"I appreciate you and your dogs helping us clear up the mystery, take them in good health. Let's climb in the car and I'll take you and the dogs home, it's been a good morning."

"I love this country; in the old country this kind of fare would be reserved for the nobs. Farmers like I was there and here, would never get a chance at game. I would like to do something with my property except farm sheep, but I'm no good with horses, cattle or pigs and I don't want to get into grain or corn, too much equipment to buy. Sheep farming is very much subsistence farming. I thought of honey, but bees kind of scare me as well."

"This morning when we picked you up, I noticed you have a lot of maple trees. You could try maple syrup that usually pays well. It also costs little to get involved with.

"Aye, I've heard of maple syrup, but I've never even tasted it. I wouldn't even know how to start."

"It's not hard, I think there is a book in the town library on it, the hard part is getting the wood together to boil the sap down, but you have lots of scrap wood on your property. It would just be a matter of gathering it up and cutting it to length. That's where the labor is. We could show you the rest, but I'll try to get that book for you, then you can better decide."

Robert, George and myself got together at the diner, when I had returned from driving McAllister and dogs home.

"That is conclusive in my opinion," said George when we all had a coffee, "I guess you could call it a betting ring in a way. I would say they are making a bundle rigging races and betting on them. How are we going to shut them down?"

"We need to get the SPCA involved as well as the racing authorities. We can have a brief talk to them tomorrow and see what they wish to do about it," said Robert

"Tomorrow is Friday and next week end we need to be at the cottage for the barbecue. Tomorrow night we have our patrols. Let's hope we have a little progress, we need to solve Sam's murder more than anything. I must say that shutting this McKenzie down will be satisfying in a way, but Sam's murder is still number one with me," I said

"I totally agree," said George, "I have a feeling that we haven't seen the last of McKenzie quite yet though. He's got some pretty violent types working for him."

"Let's leave that for now until we talk to the SPCA and the racing people, we can talk to the track manager as well tomorrow when we go to the races. Robert have you got the patrol areas laid out for us for tomorrow?"

"Yes, all ready to go, Jim will ride with you and Moishe with me. George since he has the most experience at this patrol thing will be by himself."

"Total caution this time," said George, "no one will approach any shady looking situation without radioing first and getting another one of our cars as back up to the spot. Are we all agreed on that?"

There was a round of 'Yes Sirs', while George pretended to throw his coffee at us. I went home to Mrs. MacGregor's world famous lamb with homemade mint sauce. Not as good as our own fresh caught fish in my opinion.

Friday, John had Georgian Sam in the third race a mid-range claimer. Georgian Sam won by 2 lengths after leading wire to wire. Sundown Sheila started out well but faded when it came to the stretch run.

"Oh well," said John, She's done so well all summer, it looks like she needs a bit of rest. I think I'll turn her out to pasture for a month and then bring her back for the fall racing schedule. She's more than paid for her keep this summer. I'll talk to Will when he gets her back to the barn, but I don't think there's anything wrong, just tired."

George had spoken to the police about our Mr. McKenzie's training methods and what was probably going on and they had set up an investigation. George was the perfect person to talk to them. They took him at his word literally because of his years on the force. The track manager was attentive but skeptical when I ran him to ground after the last race. He didn't believe that such a thing could be going on right under his nose, but as he pointed out, McKenzie's main operation was in Toronto. He did however tell me that he would get his security force to look into it. He would also alert the people in Toronto. I told him we would be willing to talk to them as well and tell what we knew of the things going on. He said he would tell them that and they would undoubtedly be in touch with me.

We headed for the cottage.

No burglaries had been reported on the week end. We wanted to catch a few fish to barbecue as well as arrange for the hot dogs, hamburgers and drinks. The people who had tried the barbecued fish the last time said they were delicious. Some of the neighbors had said they were bringing salads and other things like desserts. It promised to be a great party.

Wednesday night we caught three bass and two pickerel, our best catch in many days. Thursday we collected our trout lures, left Robert, much to his disgust, to make sure Mary was okay and we headed for Paul's "secret" trout stream and were rewarded with a good catch. Robert didn't like being left behind but still tired easily. That night we caught a Muskie while trolling late. Lots of fish for everyone. Friday we relaxed swimming, and generally doing nothing. Mary had made all the hamburgers and it began to look like we would be eating hamburgers for a couple of weeks to come. She said she didn't think so, we had run out last time, and this was not so many more.

We were in mid-summer and Saturday proved to be one of those days, which are brilliant and warm but not hot. People started arriving early afternoon to swim and gossip. Some had brought salads and other food and drink. Tables were set up and appetizers laid out to be slowly consumed. The barbecue was fired up and the food really started to flow. Several pies and cakes had appeared from various people. Everyone was in a good mood. Many came by to inquire about my back. It was feeling much better and I was pleased to pass on the fact. People ate both early and late snacking a little at a time all day. Everyone was stuffed. We had a great party, as evening started to settle in we settled in to dance to the radio and sing along to some of the favorite current hits. Not as good as John, Will and Dave on their instruments but everyone was enjoying themselves anyhow.

We received many compliments and were told this day had made the summer. The Keifer family as well as George had been run ragged keeping up with the crowd. Robert and I being recently hurt took it easy. As they were leaving one of our neighbors a man of about 70 obviously from Ireland came over to thank us. "Grand hoolie," he said by way of thank you. Luckily I had heard the term before, Mary came by before leaving to say she had been right, the hamburgers were gone. She was pretty astute.

Robert announced in the morning. "I think I'll see if I can get my private pilot's license. I have lots of hours in the air. I've missed it, and when we go back to the city on Monday I think I'll go to the airport and inquire about the requirements."

"That's a splendid idea," I said. "I think I've been missing it too. After the war I was glad to get away from it, but I feel that now might be the time. You know if we had a plane we could get here much faster. I own the acreage across the road. We could even get a grass strip set up there. It would be no worse than some of the one's we flew out of during the war."

"I know you two were pilots in the war, I wondered if you ever missed it," said George. "You've never mentioned it before, I thought you might have bad memories of it."

"I have bad memories attached to it," said Robert, "but we have to live as well. After the war the RAF wanted me to stay in and fly anti-submarine patrol with the Shackleton squadrons, but I just wanted a change. The threat seemed small to me, and I didn't want to fly something as big and slow."

"That's about the way I feel as well," I agreed. "Let's go into town Monday and find out what it would take to fix up the field out back. Meanwhile we can go for a walk over there to see what needs to be done."

We went for our walk right after breakfast. It was immediately clear that although the land was flat enough, it would need much under brushing done and perhaps ploughing, harrowing and rolling, as well as grass seed planting. It looked possible. George and Robert were worried about the cost. I told them not to worry, it was my problem. The main direction of the wind just happened to be the main direction of the field, but there was ample space for a cross runway for the times the wind wasn't just right.

Monday we headed to town, first to talk to Paul about who we could get to do the work. He suggested a small local firm, the owner was a friend of his and could do the work. I invited him out for Tuesday to look over what needed doing.

John called to say there had been a very violent robbery on the week end. A house had been broken into when the owner and wife were at home. The man and his wife had been bound gaged and beaten badly. There had been three of them with masks on. The house was nearly a write off. Anything of value had been stolen. It looked more and more like the gang knew where we were going to be. The whole town here had known we would be having the party. The Cavanagh kid would have certainly known. We felt sure we were on the right track.

Tuesday the small local contractor and I walked the field together. He assured me he could get it cleared with his crew this week, and the ploughing harrowing and rolling the following week. We could plant the seed for the grass this fall but we wouldn't have good grass until the following year. We would need to reseed in the spring as well. I asked him about a hanger and he said if I got some plans, he was sure he could build it.

George, Robert and I spent the rest of the day fishing. As promised, John Schell, the contractor had a crew and two tractors there on site on Wednesday morning, work had dried up in town and he was glad of the job. He got an early start. We went to Peterborough.

Chapter 14

Dave called John Sunday about 8:30 A.M, telling John that he thought that McKenzie's men may be on to him. John called me right away before church. I called Dave immediately.

"I was talking to John and he mentioned that you felt they might be getting on to you. What makes you think so?" I asked.

"I first thought nothing of it, but they moved one of their horses to a stall right across the aisle from me last week. Then yesterday one of them said 'You seem to like to watch us, so we thought we'd move closer so you could get a better view.', that's when I got to thinking that they were on to me."

"Yes I'm afraid you're right. Work today as usual. I'll call the trainer and tell him to put someone to look after Kingston Kenny for Monday and on. Pack your stuff up tomorrow and George will come and get you Monday afternoon."

"I don't think I should give up just yet, they haven't done anything, and I'm not frightened."

"I appreciate that you're willing to carry on, but these guys play rough, and I don't want you hurt. You were quite good to do this favor for me but I want to get you safe from them while we can. Don't say anything to our trainer and definitely nothing to them."

Sunday after church we settled down to one of Mrs. McGregor's prime rib roast dinners with roast potato, gravy, cauliflower, carrots and broccoli rounded out with a nice strawberry pie with whipped cream. We could hardly move we were so stuffed. The sermon had been on John 15 verses 1 to 17. 'I am the true vine'. Good sermon, good illustrations.

When we had sat down to watch "The Ed Sullivan Show", George said. "We can't quit now we are getting close. You are right in that we must now be very careful. When we are in Peterborough on the weekends, we will all have to sleep at one house and stay together no matter what. When we get back to the cottage maybe we can see if there is some other way to approach the problem."

"We'll drive to Toronto tomorrow morning pick up Dave and his things then talk to the SPCA and the racing authorities there and show them what we can about McKenzie and company. Then Tuesday or Wednesday we can go to the cottage and get some well-earned relaxation and fishing in before the week end.

"Okay by me," said Robert, "It's a lot of traveling but we have nothing better to do."

When we got to Toronto we went straight to my boarding house to pick up Dave. We were met by my other tenant. He appeared to be very upset.

"Sunday night I was sitting late with my neighbor on the porch when we saw Dave turn up the street. A couple of guys jumped him and started hitting him with baseball bats. He fell down right away and they started kicking him. We ran to help. They were big men just a couple of toughs. We had our hands full, but my neighbor across the road came to help. A cop car with two guys in it came up the street. One cop came right away, but he started to help the crooks until we yelled at him the situation. The other guy radioed for back up, then joined the fight. Even so we had a hard time holding them until the next car arrived. The police took them into custody and an ambulance came and got Dave. He was hurt but managed to get a couple of licks in.

"How is he, do you know?" I asked.

"I don't know, he told me you were coming, before they took him away. I looked for your phone number but couldn't find it. So I thought if you hadn't arrived by the time visiting hours came around, I'd go see him. They took him to St. Joseph's just down the street."

"I certainly appreciate your help. I won't forget. We'll go now and see if they'll let us see him. I'll come back after we check."

As we drove to the corner of Roncesvalles and King to the St. Joseph hospital George remarked "That bunch certainly moved fast. Who could have thought they would have already started to take action. After our visit here we'll have to stop by the police and see what they can tell us."

We arrived ten minutes before visiting hours so we sat and waited. Dave was apparently just bruised, badly in a couple of places. He also had a broken rib. That was the worst of his injuries. He would be able to go home on Tuesday. He was sore but in good spirits when we got in to see him.

"They surprised me. I wasn't expecting anything so soon. I was down before I could defend myself," Dave said

"Did you get a good look at them?" asked George.

"Oh yes, but they weren't anybody I'd seen before, maybe I was just to be a mugging victim. Maybe they were just after my wallet. They would have been disappointed, I only had two dollars on me. The police took them away anyway, so we can get a good look at them if we want to."

"Oh I think we can say with some certainty that they have some connection with McKenzie and company," replied George, "We'll go talk to the police when we leave here."

"You're allowed to go home tomorrow," I said "We'll come and get you when you're ready. Today we'll pack your things."

"I was lucky your landlord was sitting out talking, who knows what would have happened if they hadn't come to help. It was a hot night, too hot for sleeping."

"Well I guess you'll live," I said "We'll leave you now have a good sleep tonight, we'll pick you up tomorrow."

The Monday meeting with the SPCA and the racing authorities went well. We told them of all we had observed. The horses that had diarrhea were hardest to prove. Indeed they were skeptical of everything. They gave us the idea that if anything was truly happening they would have already seen it. I guess it was hard to believe, so we volunteered to show the breaking behavior. They had a Monday night card, so we said we would stay and see if we could point out anything. We consulted Dave and found out that there was a possibility that night. The race in question was a middle class claimer where a horse McKenzie trained would likely be favorite. Since the winning purse would not be large, it was an opportunity for them to nobble the horse and make more on the betting end. We went and talked to the racing authorities about the possibility. They agreed to watch with us. Just before the race the second favorite was scratched, on investigation the horse was found to have severe diarrhea. It looked as if the fix was under way. We got the racing people to sit with us close to the McKenzie people. When the race was being run we made sure they watched the McKenzie crowd closely. Sure enough the favorite, their horse, broke coming down the stretch and lost to a long odds outsider. Just as the horse broke we pointed out that one of McKenzie's men had put something to his mouth and we could see him blowing. The McKenzie men were in high good humour as we followed them to the tote for their payout. The racing authorities were quite grim, but said nothing. They said they would get back to us. We had a sleep and headed to pick up Dave and return home so that we could head for the cottage tomorrow for some fishing action.

Driving home Dave said, "Why do people do things like that?"

"Do you mean, race fixing," I asked.

"Yes all the things they do to get a winner or a winning bet."

"Well its greed mostly, and power to some extent," I said. "Unfortunately the horse racing industry is sort of a perfect business to attract that sort of thing. A person can make a decent living training and racing horses and if a person has a really good memory and is very smart you can make a living even betting on horses but that's not a combination you find very often in a bettor. All gamblers think they have it, but the vast majority aren't as smart as they think they are. Most lose all the money they can lay their hands on and still don't learn. Most resort to cheating in some way. It's best just to play it straight. That's not the glamorous way, but it's the only sure way."

"I guess I never thought about that, but now that you've mentioned it, that makes sense. I'll have to think about it a lot."

"If you want to talk about it at any time, just ask."

We got to the cottage early Wednesday morning and Paul came out late afternoon and had supper with us. He was in a way not surprised by the news of the robbery. He knew what James Cavanagh was capable of. The horse racing was foreign to him, but understandable. He had also thought of a way we might be able to find out something from James' girlfriend. He had met an old friend in town at church. She was a cousin to James' girlfriend's mother and visited them quite often. She too was well aware of James's violence, her own daughter had been assaulted by James just before the war. Her daughter had managed to escape. James only managed to miss having a term in jail by going into the army. Paul felt he could approach his friend and brief her about what we needed, she could be our best bet at getting the information we were looking for. We were worried about whether Cavanagh would hear of the questions being asked, but Paul was adamant that it was the best way, so we told him to go ahead and see what she could get. An address would be nice but any information was a help. This James Cavanagh was getting nervous, which made him even more dangerous. We were closing in. We all went for a nice cruise around the lake then a short fishing expedition.

John called to say that Kingston Kenny had developed a bad case of diarrhea. His Toronto trainer had taken the horse out to his farm in Markham to recover. His grooms had seen the Mackenzie grooms hanging around Kingston Kenny's stall but that was not too unusual because they had a horse in a close by stall. The vet felt the cause had been something my horse had eaten but wasn't sure. The vet had got the diarrhea under control and my horse should be fully recovered by the next day. John wanted to know what to do about things. I said I thought it was time we gave Kingston Kenny a rest anyhow, so why not bring him back to John's barn where he would be home. John agreed and said he would sent Will down to pick him up this week. Until things settled down I felt much better having my horses where they would be best guarded and looked after.

We headed for Peterborough first light Friday morning. Mrs. MacGregor was glad to see us. She was informed of our plans and said she would make a nice supper for us. She put our fish in the freezer and started on a nice roast beef supper for when we got back. Meanwhile we called Jim Martin, Moishe and John and invited everyone for dinner courtesy of Mrs. MacGregor. After lunch we went out to the golf course. We hadn't golfed in a couple of weeks now, as a group we hadn't all been healthy. We tired quickly, even though we just had lunch and walked around a bit, so we returned to our house and while Robert had a nap George and I played two handed euchre. The result proved that neither of

us had an advantage at the game, our skill level was about equal.
Dinner was a huge success, Mrs. MacGregor had outdone herself
and even had two blueberry cream pies for dessert. She was a good
person and worked hard and willingly. Moishe and Jim stayed for a
while and we brought them up to date on our progress. Moishe was
elated, he felt the same as us, and we were getting close to Sam's
murderer.

John had two horses running Friday and two Saturday. We
hadn't been to the races much lately either, so we planned to
go both nights. I hadn't had a chance yet to talk to him about
my wish to buy a stud to stand at his farm. He was overjoyed
at the news and said he would keep an eye open for a prospect.
Sundown Sheila, John's good mare was running Friday as well
as Jake Sheldrake's Sim's Delight. My gelding, Dorset Lightning
was on Saturday night with one of Jake Sheldrake's other horses.
Paul called to say that all they had gained was the fact that, two
others were living with James and it was in a farmhouse near
Peterborough, location unknown. That mostly confirmed what we
knew, there were three of them. They were not right in the city by
the sound of it, which made it harder to find them.

"I wonder why people go bad?" began Robert. "Take this
fellow Cavanagh, he didn't have to do the things he has done."

"That's the $64,000 question, some people just become desperate, and desperate people do desperate things. That's not the case here though, this guy is just evil. As trite as it seems I think it just all relates back to the Bible, and the commandments. It seems like Satan just puts a demon into some people. That's more like the case with this Cavanagh fellow." said George. "He had a poor upbringing it seems, but with his eye, he could have been an Olympic champion marksman. There wasn't much of a chance though, not with his background."

"Some people are just dumb," said George, "take the guy who started working weekends and late into the night on a secret project."

"Here we go," said Robert.

"Anyway," continued George, "after months of work he went to his friend Josh, to show him the fruits of his labor. "Check this out," he said. "I made it." And he proudly showed his buddy a seventeen dollar bill.

It's a beautiful counterfeit," said his buddy Josh admiringly, "But you're never going to get anywhere with a seventeen dollar bill."

Oh, yeah?" says the guy furiously. "Just wait!" He runs down to the deli on the corner. A few minutes later he came back beaming from ear to ear.

"Well?' said Josh

"Told you they'd give me change," he declared proudly. "Look two seven dollar bills and a three."

"I get the point," I said "Dumb can be a characteristic, but I don't think this guy is very dumb, He's more arrogant than dumb."

"And quite violent in the bargain," finished George.

After lunch we headed to Morrow Park. John's horse was in the third race a race for non-winners of three races in the past 60 days. She had won two so was a class higher today. John still felt she had a decent chance. Sim's Delight was in the seventh. We ran into Harry White the track manager as we were entering. "Got something running tonight?" he asked, "I haven't seen you guys in ages."

"No, "I said "John has some runners so we just came to watch and cheer them on, we've been up to the cottage and have missed coming. I have a horse tomorrow."

"Good luck with him, perhaps well see you tomorrow. We could have a coffee together if I can get the time," said Harry

Ralph Davidge was there as usual. Three sheets to the wind, also as usual. "How are you fellows and your horses today," he yelled in passing.

"Very well thanks Ralph," I replied.

Robert said mildly, "He's not a bad man. I can see your thinking of trying to get him off the sauce, but it's going to be a long haul I think."

"Probably, but once he was an effective member of the community, He's had some bad breaks."

The third race came up quickly, Sundown Sheila ran well, she led most of the way but faded to third in a photo.

"Good race!" said Robert. "She only lost by a total of half a length, and she set the pace and did all the work. She'll win at this level."

"She did look good," said George thoughtfully, "You know I might just get a cheap claimer to race for something to shout at."

"That would be fun," I said.

We went for a break, a coffee and a hot dog. We didn't need the hot dog, Mrs. MacGregor was feeding us well. It was just something to fortify ourselves for the night. Sim's Delight pulled up lame, he had thrown a splint. He would be out of racing for a while. Jake Sheldrake would not be pleased.

Saturday, Ralph again met us on the way in. He seemed more sober than usual. Kurt was nearby watching the crowd come in, "Good evening Mr. Withers" he said. "Got a runner today?"

"Yes, thank you," I replied. "Dorset Lightning in the seventh."

"Good luck," he called.

Dorset Lightning started off well but got boxed in on the rail and couldn't get out until the winner had crossed the finish line. So much for this week.

We left to meet Jim and Moishe for our rounds. George would be by himself, Jim with me and Moishe with Robert. We briefed the two newcomers on the use of the radio. They would be the communicators, George would be his own operator. The hours dragged. We saw nothing. We kept up a running dialog mostly to keep awake. Too many of us had been stressed to far lately.

Monday we stayed in Peterborough to do some flying for our licenses. The weather was beautiful. Robert and I both passed our licensing easily. We would have to wait a while before flying our IFR (Instrument Flight Rules) tests but at least we could fly at the moment when the weather was nice and the clouds were above the limits laid down for Visual Flight Rules (VFR). We both had many hours of IFR in the Air force, but government rules were to be followed so we would wait. It would be frustrating but such is life.

Robert again visited the hanger were the Druine Turbulent was being built and declared he would like to build a replica of the Spitfire he had flown in the War. We didn't know if plans were available to do that, but Robert being an engineer felt he could draw up something. That sounded pretty ambitious to me. Happy on the progress on that front Robert, George and I retired to the golf course for a round.

The golf was about the same as when we had started out the year. We'd been busy, no practicing. We'd got rusty. An easy thing to do with golf.

"We'll have to get back to practicing," declared Robert. He was quite passionate about his game.

Chapter 15

We went for a drive to John's farm to see how things were going. Robert and George had decided they would like to get into the racing in a minor way.

"I guess we'll know in a couple of years if Kingston Kenny has the goods to be a stud. Your slow mare, Betty's Dream, is definitely pregnant," said John, as he came out to meet us. "We'll have a foal early spring next year then wait another year and a half and we'll start to see if it's a runner."

"Can you look around for a good but inexpensive horse for me to buy in the near future," said George."

"Has the racing bug bitten you now," replied John.

"I think it would be neat to run against one of Bill's horses," said George

"You had better get two then, about the same ability as I don't have anything like that just now," I said. "That'll give you two more horses for those new stalls."

"Better make that three," added Robert.

"Happy to help, particularly when it makes me more money."

That settled we proceeded to the airport. Many courses were available for an Instrument rating plus night endorsement, Dual

engine and anything else we might want. We asked about aircraft
sales and were directed to another office. The salesman was in
and willing to talk. We discussed what was available as new and
used. There was a bewildering array of planes in the catalogs per
company. Cessna and Piper were the biggest list, with Beech and
others as well. The salesman suggested Cessna or Piper would be
best as first class mechanics were available on site but while others
could be serviced, the mechanics were always up to date here on
the two main makes. There were some small Cessna's available
for rental on site, but while they could easily get us to the cottage
in about a half hour, I was more interested in something faster
that could fly further. I was thinking we could stretch our fishing
excursions further in all directions.

We took the brochures home to review them and talk it over
with Robert. The Cessna 310 right away caught my eye. It was
not the cheapest but gave good speed and endurance to fly almost
anywhere we would like to go. Robert and I looked over the
brochures carefully. George was also an interested party. The
Cessna 310 wound up as my choice. With twin 240 horse power
engine and fuel enough for 1000 nautical miles range at a cruising
speed of 205 nautical miles per hour, we would be able to go a
good distance at a good speed. Others in the same price range were

not as fast or had less range or both. We talked about the good and

bad points, George was still trying to save me money, pointing out

that there were cheaper airplanes. Robert liked the specifications,

but was still stuck on the fighters we had flown in the war. The

money was no problem, so we settled on this one. Since it would

be new it had all the up to date instruments which would be a little

new to us both. We would need most of the courses available to

handle this baby, but we were confident we could handle a craft

like this eventually.

That evening for our patrol, Jim and I were together, Jim

driving, George by himself and Moishe with Robert. About two

in the morning I spotted what I thought was some movement

of shadows near a house that was all in darkness. I radioed the

address to the other cars, waited a few seconds then Jim got out

and slowly headed to the house, perhaps they didn't know there

were two of us in the car. I slid behind the wheel, ready for action.

The other cars were on the way. George was to pull into the street

that ran behind the house, Robert headed for us, he was furthest

away. Jim turned the corner of the house and immediately was

rushed by the gang. Contact. I swung the car around and headed

it into the driveway as well. When the lights swung that way two

people left Jim and headed for the rear. Same tactic. I radioed to

George and he replied he was close. George drove into the street but too late they were gone. He drove hard to the next intersection, but nothing was visible. Very close this time, they had been ready for us. One of them must have been waiting in the pickup. Even so a few seconds more and we would have had them. We held a conference, but the only thing we could think of was that the Cavanagh kid in Bobcaygeon must have warned them we would be patrolling. At this point there was no need to keep the patrol going for the rest of the night. We headed to my house to get some rest. Nothing again.

Sunday at church, it was evident the secretary was back. The bulletin read, "The eighth-graders will be presenting Shakespeare's Hamlet in the Church basement Friday at 7 PM. The congregation is invited to attend this tragedy." Well at least some things never seemed to change.

Monday we went to the airport, to book test rides and other courses we felt would be of use and interest. The salesman nearly fell over us when I told him that we were considering the Cessna 310. I guessed that it might be the best sale he would get all year. They didn't have one on site but would get one flown up from the factory for my approval by next Saturday. The aircraft would be complete with all the bells and whistles, including a factory representative to give us a test flight. I rented a Cessna 170 to

get us back and forth to the cottage for a while. The salesman

said if I purchased the aircraft there would be a couple of months

wait for delivery. I asked about hangers or plans for hangers. He

explained we could easily get space here, I had meant something

for the cottage. Anything he suggested for that was too expensive

to contemplate. I felt certain we could design something better

ourselves.

We reported the close call we had to the police, how near we

had come. All of us felt we were getting closer to Sam's murderer.

After finishing our chores around Peterborough, we headed to the

cottage. It took us over an hour. Robert commented that we could

do it faster henceforth as we could get there in less than half an

hour by the plane. We would take charge of the rental 170 next

Saturday. George would drive his car to the cottage after next

weekend so we would have wheels at the cottage. We were all

surprised to see how well our landing strip was coming along. We

had a short swim and headed into the lake in the small runabout.

It was pleasant just quietly trolling. The night was beautiful, a full

moon was shining and we could see many stars. The lake was

always so quiet when the water skiers had given up for the day,

particularly during the week when many of the rowdies had gone back to work. We even caught two medium sized pickerel. It was a good thing we all enjoyed fish.

We relaxed on the veranda before bed, we had experienced a satisfying day.

Robert said thoughtfully, "I could maybe go to Peterborough early, maybe on the bus. I could pick up the 170 early, fly here about 6 PM and pick up the rest. We could then fly to Peterborough and do our patrol. We could leave the car here and they might think we were here rather than there and we could maybe catch them napping. If we made a visit into town late afternoon to advertise our presence here they would never know we were in Peterborough."

"That's a good thought," said George. "Let's see tomorrow what the bus schedule happens to be. Trouble is we might be seen getting on the bus and they could think something was up."

"They don't know me very well though," said Robert

"Good thoughts guys," I said "Let's sleep on it and maybe add to and revise it tomorrow. I'm bushed."

Tuesday I called John Schell and asked him to come out so we could discuss a hanger. The field itself was in good shape. There had been many stones to be removed but, this they had accomplished over the weekend. It was already ploughed, harrowed and rolled, this bunch moved fast.

Mary arrived, I could see right away that something was wrong. She had been crying. "What's wrong?" I asked

"It's Ray Cavanagh," she said, "he pushed Ken my boyfriend into a fight on the weekend, of course he didn't fight fair even though he's bigger and stronger than Ken. He had his friends interfere with anything Ken tried to do, like catch his fist when he tried to fight back or trip him. Ray kicked him several times when he fell. They beat him quite badly, he's at home in town with broken ribs and a lot of bruises. His dad says he'll be alright. We reported it to the police and they went out to arrest Ray, but he claims Ken started it and he just fought back. His friends say they had nothing to do with it but admit they were there and Ken started it. The police have nothing to go on. Ken says Ray demanded Ken stay away from me or he would get more of the same, or worse. What can we do?"

"Well I think this Cavanagh thing is going to come to a head very shortly," I said, "it may be best to just lay low for a couple of weeks until we get it sorted out, but make sure you stay well away from this Cavanagh boy. Don't go anywhere alone. He's a sneaky fellow. I'll see if I can get through to him, but it isn't likely, he's getting bolder."

"Somebody is always with me when I'm out here working and Ken and I can stay home for a while, but when school starts it will be difficult."

"That's still two or three weeks away, hopefully we'll have it solved by then."

John Schell arrived, so we sat down to discuss what we would be needing for a hanger. Starting with the dimensions of the plane, we added onto it for a large workshop at the back. The front would have a door most of the width of the building, that raised up to the ceiling to allow the plane to be put in. John said he knew a guy in town that had an Architectural degree. He would talk to this fellow, price everything out, then we talk again. Meanwhile the weather was nice and it would be awhile before I took delivery of the new plane.

I drove to town with George. We found Ray Cavanagh with his side kicks, lounging around their usual haunts.

"What do you want old man?" he asked as George and I approached.

"You can't seem to stay out of trouble. Do you have a wish to spend most of your life behind bars, or worse?"

"I wouldn't be so uppity old man. You've had a warning, I understand. Worse could be coming."

I turned to the two sidekicks and said. "Hanging out with this fellow is going to get you two in a lot of trouble, I'd think twice about things if I were you. As for you Mr. Cavanagh you no doubt think you got away with something this weekend, but I'll tell you once more, and this is the last warning. "Back off.", you're going to be watched closely hereafter and pretending the problem has nothing to do with you isn't going to work."

He laughed loudly, his sidekicks did as well. "There is nothing you can do, if you try we'll fix you good."

"Well no doubt you can beat me up. Some young guy who isn't a coward like you could probably do that. Even so I bet you wouldn't try without your stooges holding me. If you kill me you'll hang. You two as well for being accessories. If you don't kill me you better be prepared to run fast and far. That's not a threat but a solemn promise."

He took a couple of threatening steps toward me. "You better get out of here old man, or you'll get it right here."

He came right up nose to nose, I didn't back up, just stood and looked into his eyes, and hoped I showed no fear. I felt none, George hadn't moved either.

He said to his friends. "This old man is bugging me lets go for a drive, fellows," With that they got into their car and drove away.

"You certainly take chances," said George as they departed.

"Those sort of people are all around us, but if you back down once, they keep after you forever," I said.

"That's true," said George, "but being an ex-policeman, I can tell you it's dangerous."

"You're probably right," I said, "but I don't wish to live in fear of his kind for the rest of my life either."

We got some supplies and headed back to the cottage. When we were driving back I said to George, "You know I wonder if he's tipping off his brother, when we are in Peterborough and when we're here. It has to be his brother. Did you hear what he said back there? He told me I had been warned. The only person that's given me any kind of warning, has been the guy who whipped me."

"Yes," said George "It would be easy to drive out past the cottage and see when we're there then call his brother to tell him the coast is clear. Then his brother knows he doesn't need to take extra precautions."

"You know that sounds about right, his brother Jimmy and his gang seem to use an unrestricted approach when we're up here."

"I've been thinking about what Robert suggested, it sounds better the more I think of it," I said, "It's about time we turned the tables on that, if it is happening. Let's set them up, let them have some false information about where we are and when, it would make our job in Peterborough much easier I think."

"That sounds like a really good idea," said George with enthusiasm, "You always seem to have such good thoughts. Let's get out to the cottage and kick some ideas around with the others."

We all got together around the table for a council of war. When we assembled I hesitated for a couple of seconds, and so George jumped in with, "Your mind sometimes works like lightning. One brilliant flash and it is gone."

"You must be feeling frisky today, you're back to the jokes, are you saying I'm just a flash in the pan," I said. I explained what George and I had been discussing, "What we need to do is something to make the Cavanagh kid think we're still here, but actually we need to be in Peterborough to do the patrols. If we leave the car here, we'll have to use the airplane to get back to Peterborough to do the patrols."

"I think the bus is best," suggested Robert.

Not a bad idea," said George, "but they may see us getting on to the bus."

"How about this," said Paul, "if you don't mind driving my old jalopy to Peterborough on Friday, you could leave your car here. I could get a couple of friends to come and stay here for Friday and Saturday, to make it look like you're here for the weekend. We would have to stay inside, but we could do that. It would sort of be like going to a hunting camp, with bad weather set in. We could play cards and talk to pass the time, then the lights would be on as usual and the car would be out front to advertise the fact that you fellows were here. We could get some food in, I'm a fair cook, as long as we swapped cars Friday somewhere that they wouldn't see us, I'm sure we could manage it."

"Brilliant," said George.

"I could get in some T-bone steaks, baking potatoes, and all the fixings for Friday night, what would you like for your main meal Saturday?" I asked.

"You don't need to do that," said Paul, "We can bring something."

"It's the least I can do. Talk to your friends and see what they say, we'll see if we can get a couple of fish for your Saturday meal, there is a lot of other stuff here and you can use any of it. That sounds like a brilliant plan as George says."

We were all agreed so the meeting broke up and we went to town for a game of golf while Paul took Mary home and went to talk to his buddies.

As we walked the golf course we refined our plans somewhat.

"Let's call the Airport in Peterborough and ask if we can pick up the 170," said Robert. "Then I could fly back here after taking the old car down there and nobody would be the wiser."

"When we get to Peterborough, we still have Paul's old car for the patrolling, but we better stay hidden and not go to the race track, golf course or airport. They might be watching for us, particularly at the track," said Robert.

"That's an excellent idea," replied George. "We just keep our heads down and just make our move late Saturday night. We should also tell the police our plan, maybe they can add a squad car or two, for that night at least. I think they can tune to our radio frequencies well enough and they could listen in to our conversation, and co-ordinate the effort."

"I think, this time we may be on to something good," I said. "I have a good feeling about our chances to run down Sam's murderer with this plan."

"Let's hope so," said George, "it's been a long frustrating summer. We suffered at their hands, I feel it's finally our turn."

"Our turn was bound to come around sooner or later."

Chapter 16

Friday morning, we drove into Bobcaygeon to let ourselves be seen. We deliberately drove by were Ray and his cronies who were hanging out at their usual haunt. Then unhurriedly we drove back toward the cottage were we met up with Paul and swapped cars. Robert got in the jalopy and headed to Peterborough to get the aircraft. He was to lay low at his house when he got there and arrange to pick up the Cessna 170 early Saturday afternoon. We settled down to play cards until Robert returned Saturday in the Cessna. Paul proved to be the best card player.

"I hope something positive comes out of this week-end," said George. "It's getting frustrating, not that I think we should give up, but the police will have started to move on from Sam's murder case."

"Yes, no doubt they have other priorities coming up," I said. "I do think this is our best bet so far. We'll catch them napping, you'll see."

"I like the way you fellows operate," said Paul. "I know if I'd been murdered I'd like to think someone kept after the creeps responsible."

"I know how the police operate they can't continue on one case forever when other things happen all the time, to take their attention. Besides I liked Sam very much," said George.

"We'll keep going if this doesn't work," I said, "But I have a good feeling about this week-end, I also liked Sam."

Robert called to say he had arrived home, there didn't seem to be anybody watching his house and the 170 was set to go for tomorrow.

Finally we retired to our beds to sleep the sleep of the just.

Robert arrived in the 170 about 1:30 P.M. Saturday. The flight had only taken half an hour. The landing field at the cottage was nowhere near finished, but he had landed on much worse during the war. He was elated. We three hopped in my car and went to make an appearance to the Cavanagh kid and his cronies. They were in their usual spot, so we made sure they saw us without appearing too brazen. Then back to the cottage to get our equipment. We hopped in the plane and headed for Peterborough in good spirits.

On arrival at my house, we drove the old jalopy around to the back of the house where it couldn't be seen from the street. George and Robert's cars were in the drive were we had left them. We carefully went inside, called the police and described our plan. Mrs MacGregor declared that she had seen something bad happening over the weekend. She said she felt we were walking into a bad situation and asked us to be very careful. We promised that we would take more care than we ever had on previous patrols. We called Moishe and Jim as well as a friend of George's to help with the patrol, which would give us two people to each car. Mrs. MacGregor treated us to a nice rack of lamb, with all the trimmings as usual. This topped off with a slice of homemade apple pie, made us quite drowsy as we relaxed in front of the television to watch the news.

"Nothing much on tonight"" observed Robert, "how about a game of whist?"

Both George and I answered at the same time. "Sounds good to me."

We had three games then headed off to bed for a short nap

Just before we were ready to go out, George appeared nervous. Being an ex-policeman, you wouldn't think confrontation would get him nervous, but at these times you could count on a joke, and sure enough, he didn't disappoint he said.

"A friend was in front of me coming out of church one day, and the preacher was standing at the door as he always is to shake hands. He grabbed my friend by the hand and pulled him aside. The Pastor said to him, "You need to join the Army of the Lord!" My friend replied, "I'm already in the Army of the Lord, Pastor."

Pastor questioned, "How come I don't see you except at Christmas and Easter?"

He whispered back, "I'm in the secret service."

At least we'll start off relaxed I thought, we had our laugh and started for the cars. Jim, Moishe and George's friend had just showed up. We were off. George with his friend, Robert with Moishe, with Jim and me in the old jalopy. We checked our radios to make sure they were working well, and checked in with the police as well.

It was about 2:00 AM that Robert reported a pickup truck, that looked to be the same one as before, outside a darkened house, but there were lights showing inside that looked to be coming from a flashlight. We got the address and headed there. The police co-coordinator reported that he was sending a patrol car our way and to just stand by. We parked quietly just up the street. We were second to arrive with George close behind. Within two minutes the patrol car came speeding around the corner with all lights flashing and the siren screaming like a banshee. So much for the quiet approach. The suspects came running out of the house, as the policeman piled out of his cruiser. A shot rang out and the policeman seemed to stop suddenly. He slumped to the ground as the pickup took off hurriedly up the road. Robert and Sam said they would stay with the patrolman, George and I took off after the pickup. George in hot pursuit, with us, Jim driving, following as we could in the old car. We could hear Robert telling the coordinator what had happened and asking for an ambulance. The young patrolman was in bad shape but holding on. Moishe had a pressure bandage on the wound, and had managed to staunch the flow of blood. We relayed as soon as we could get the line free, where we were, and which way we were headed.

The police had given us the okay to use the police frequency if we got into a problem. I told them what was happening. They had one patrol car to the east of us. The pickup was traveling at a great rate of speed. George lost them, but reported they had swung east. Great, the patrolman was in that direction. Apparently the patrolman picked them up but we heard nothing for a long while. The patrolman finally radioed that he had them pinned down in a farm house to the east. Then a distress call, saying he had been hit by gunfire. We headed as fast as we could in that direction. More police were also on the way. We arrived first, the patrolman had lost a lot of blood, an ambulance had been dispatched. The criminals tried to flee. It appeared they had grabbed what they could and tried to head out. The only way out appeared to be out the driveway. The cruiser blocked it partially, so I quickly blocked the rest with Paul's jalopy. We ran across to the other ditch, taking the wounded man with us. Several shots came our way, but we were lucky. Since the bank of the road was too high, they had no way out, they came up the driveway fast and hit the jalopy as it seemed like the easiest way through. They didn't make it, so they climbed out and scrambled back into the house. We had nothing to detain them, but George had kept his radio, so he informed the police coordinator of our situation. We patched up the patrolman's wounds as best we could and waited. Two other patrol car from the police arrived in a very short while, one headed up a side lane to block off the back of the house. We had flushed them, but now it was serious business. Police didn't like people firing shots at them, especially a deadly sniper, and when one of them was wounded they became very intense. The senior officer headed for the house but cautioned us to stay clear. They wanted to get as many finger prints as possible. We explored around but stayed well away from the buildings. The principal officer from the OPP arrived and took over with one of his minions taking our statements, more complete ones would need to be done later. It appeared at the last report that the first young patrolman who had been hurt, was likely to survive. In part by the efforts of Moishe and Robert. We headed home to sleep. We were exhausted.

Over the rest of the night, it was a standoff. Near morning
a negotiation was started between the burglars and the police.
The police found out how deadly the robbers were by getting
themselves a couple of more wounded officers. The situation had
settled down to a siege, the police certainly would not give up.
They had some wounded officers, and they had the thieves run
to ground. Negotiations went on through the day. It was the lead
story on all the radio stations, and by nightfall, the television
news had picked it up as their lead story as well. We called the
police and told them we would be in to complete our statements
after church. The secretary had struck yet again, she had written
in the bulletin, "The sermon this morning: 'Jesus Walks on the
Water.' The sermon next Sunday: 'Searching for Jesus.'" The whole
congregation gathered around us, after church, while we had coffee
in the basement. They were all looking avidly for more details. We
told them what we could, they made us out to be heroes. We didn't
feel like heroes, but we had a certain sense of accomplishment. It
looked like we had helped to run Sam's killers to earth.

After lunch at home we all went to the police station to
complete our statements. We were told how things were standing
out at the siege. It had settled down to a waiting game big
floodlights were being brought in, it looked as if they were not

going to get things wrapped up before nightfall. No other injuries had occurred but shots were being fired every so often to try to keep the thieves awake. I called Paul to tell him about the fate of his car. I promised him he would not suffer by it, it was my responsibility as it was I who decided to place it in harm's way. I would get a replacement for him Monday. He was upset because he didn't want charity as he put it, but I insisted, he had to admit he couldn't afford a new one, I asked him if he would feel better if I got him a used car as a replacement. In the end he agreed to a used one. He said he, and his friends had a great weekend and asked if I minded them staying over until we arrived. He had settled down to the inevitable and thanked me for thinking about him, and his car. I told him he was quite welcome to stay, I would consider it a problem solved as we wouldn't be back until Monday afternoon at the earliest.

I picked up Ralph and we went home to a huge Sunday victory dinner, Mrs. MacGregor had been assisted by Mrs. Wilson and Mrs. Johnson. We all ate too much. They had a beautiful roast of beef with Yorkshire pudding, roast potatoes, carrots, corn and cabbage. Mrs. MacGregor loved cabbage. There was a cake and two pies, one apple, one blueberry. The blueberries were fresh picked. Mrs Wilson made sure Ralph ate a good size meal. She had remembered that when she was young, she had been a friend of the girl that had become Ralph's wife. They sat together and discussed old times. We stopped eating when we were stuffed, John had come and so had Moishe, Jim and George's friend. It was a big crowd probably the first time ever my huge old oak dining room table had been this full. No one felt like fun and games afterward, the only topic of conversation was the impending arrest of our summer's problem makers. We were very relieved to have a successful conclusion to a summer of pain and suffering. We had been battered but had persevered.

Monday we woke up to a busy day, we took possession of the Cessna and Robert would fly it north to the cottage that afternoon. George and I went first to a neighbor's house to look at a car he had. It was a two year old Chevy Delray, a new model in 1954, my neighbor liked to buy a new car every two years. He never drove far, but he had a cousin with a GM dealership. The car was in top shape with very little mileage on it, and he was only asking $800.00 dollars. It appeared to be a bargain, so I went to the bank and got the money for it. I called my insurance agent and set up insurance on it. Once all was arranged, George and I picked up Ralph and started for the cottage. Next weekend was Labor Day, and we had previously set up for our last barbecue for the summer. The usual crowd was invited. We needed to get supplies in for it, immediately. I was feeling in a really good mood, as we had finally run the robbers to ground so I bought enough T-bone steaks to supply everybody that wanted one. The grocery in Bobcaygeon didn't have enough on hand but would have them ready for us on Saturday morning. Paul took one look at the car and shook his head

"That's much better than my old car," he said. "I couldn't take that."

"Don't be upset," I said, "I got it for a really good price from my neighbor, who trades in his car every two years, and besides you helped us greatly by keeping the cottage safe as well as the other things you've done for us this summer. Look at it as payment for services rendered. Also, who showed us the best trout fishing water, you did! These waters have given us a lot of pleasure this summer. Pretend it's a Christmas present or whatever. Just please take it, to humor me if nothing else."

"Well you are far to kind," said Paul, "but I guess I do need some transportation, it's just that I've never had such a good car before."

"You deserve it," I replied. "Look at all the help your family has given us at our parties and so on. We'll need you again this week end."

It was easy to see he'd like to take it, he had a huge grin on his face, but being old fashioned he didn't like feeling he was taking charity.

I passed him the keys and told him to take it for a spin, he could drive his buddies back to town. They had a great time over the weekend eating, playing card games and just hanging around.

Robert arrived just before they left, so we all trouped across the road to see our new mode of travel. He made a perfect landing with the 170 and taxied up to the roadside end of the landing area. We offered to take Paul and his two buddies for a little ride. They were a bit shy, but eventually we talked them into it. They climbed in and Robert took off, they came back 45 minutes later, they had been over Bobcaygeon and had even flown over Fenelon Falls, Burnt River, and Kinmount. I could see that they would be talking of nothing else in town for a few days. Robert had certainly given them a good ride.

We retired to the cottage. I decided I would leave my car here during the week and fly back and forth to Peterborough. I could get a new car for home. It was about time, my old car was starting to have a few problems anyway. Robert, George, Ralph and me went fishing for the evening, then listened to the news on the radio. The weather was looking good, hopefully it would stay that way for the long week end and our barbecue. We caught no fish that night, but we were in too good a mood to let that ruin our return to the cottage, in triumph. The news that was of any interest to us was mainly sports items. There was a brief story about the siege in

Peterborough, it was still a standoff but the police felt certain that they would be able to bring it to a close the next day.

The baseball season was winding down. It looked like the best two teams were both in New York this year with the Yankees holding sway in the American league and the Brooklyn Dodgers in the National, although the Milwaukee Braves and Cincinnati Reds were giving them a run for their money. The National Hockey League training camps were also due to open soon, with Montreal seen as the early favorites to repeat. There was also a lot of talk about the new rule for the coming year. To try to even things up a little, the powers had decided that a 2 minute penalty would end if the team with the power play scored. In previous years the team that had the best power play could score as many times as they could in a two minute penalty. The Peterborough Petes were probably already at camp. They had been the Kitchener Canucks, the previous year. We felt we should support the home town team, so we decided to get season tickets.

Tuesday we took advantage of Paul's good trout fishing stream and returned home with 4 good size ones. Robert the expert had caught two. Mary told us how her grandfather was in second heaven with his new car and his first airplane ride the previous day. Robert offered to take her for a ride after lunch. Paul came out shortly after lunch in his new car, as proud as a peacock, so he got his second ride in an aircraft with Mary going as well. They flew pretty much the same route as the day before. George, Ralph and I went after some bass for the afternoon.

Wednesday, we went to the driving range for a bucket of balls each then to the golf club for a round. We had missed the golf, we usually went more often than we had this summer. Ralph came along to watch, our skills had eroded from the earlier good scores we had enjoyed, but we had a pleasant time anyway. The news that night said the siege in Peterborough was over, the three men arrested in an exhausted condition. Jimmy Cavanagh, was said to be defiant. One of the others, had been injured when they had crashed into our car trying to escape. The police praised our efforts. We only felt relief. We felt we had only been trying to get some retribution for our murdered friend Sam.

Chapter 17

Thursday, after rising late, we had a leisurely swim while Mary cleaned, Paul had driven her out, but headed back to town. Mary told us how proud her grandfather was of the car, and how proud he was of the help he had been able to give us. He was probably at the coffee shop or the barber's shop telling of the results of the investigation.

At lunch time we headed to town, to have our favorite, the pork chop lunch at the diner. When we came out of the diner, Ray Cavanagh came storming up to confront us.

"You were told to keep your nose out of other people's business. Now you've got my brother thrown in jail. You'll be sorry!"

"I think you're laboring under a misconception young fellow," I said. "It's definitely not my fault your brother finds himself behind bars. You can't steal and hurt people and expect people to just let you do what you want. The ten commandments aren't multiple choice, nor are they two orders and eight suggestions."

He advanced to me until he was nose to nose, his face was scarlet, his manner very threatening. Don't show any fear I said to myself. He frightens me but I can't let it show. George and Robert moved closer. "You better be watching over your shoulder old man. I'll fix you one of these days. You won't even see me coming."

"You're being very foolish, unless you're determined to wind up where your brother is, I'd do some hard thinking if I were you."

He and his friends stormed away.

"Maybe we better think of something to do about him," said George, "He's dangerous, let's put our minds to it after the Labor Day holiday. There's Mary to think of too, she kind of depends on us to an extent to keep him away from her as well. She has to go back to school next week, and she'll be more vulnerable there. Her boyfriend will be as well."

"I agree, that was very unfunny," said Robert.

On our return to the cottage, we called the police to relate the incident. They told us that Jimmy Cavanagh was maintaining that he had killed no one. Other than that they had him cold, he was going to spend a long time behind bars, at the very least.

"You know," I said to Robert and George, "maybe he didn't do it."

"He must have," said Robert," who else could it have been?"

"Ron has a point," said George, "it certainly points toward him, but there is no real evidence. He wounded two policemen and they'll hold that against him, in a big way, but we'll have to have a think on it and see if we can come up with some hard facts to connect him or he may get away with it."

"Let's go do a little fishing to finish off the day. He'll keep, he isn't going anywhere for a while. After the week end we'll sit down to a discussion for both problems. Let's leave them until then. It seems we haven't solved anything yet, but we're closing in on it."

We went fishing, and although we weren't trying very hard we caught a nice pickerel anyway. The summer had been intense. There was a couple of days of just relaxation until the final barbecue. Most of our neighbors would be heading back to their various cities, until next year. Robert and I took turns flying the 170. We showed George the basics, he said that he might sign up for lessons over the winter. We flew to Muskoka and back one day. There was a huge airport there from the war days. Another day we flew to Lindsay and back. We were getting the old skills back.

Robert and George went fishing Friday night. Ralph and I relaxed on the veranda, it was a clear warm night. "How are you feeling Ralph," I asked, "you've done well, it's been over a week without a drink? You don't seem to be missing it too badly. I did notice a bit of the shakes, but you seem to be holding up well."

"As you say, Ron, it's not easy, I've been wanting a drink badly. I tried not to show it, but I've felt very sick at times. I think I'd like

to quit, but I don't know if I could do it. It's been a long time since
I even thought of doing anything else."

"I was told about you losing both your wife and your son. That
must have been hard to endure."

Ralph broke down at that point, the tears rolling down his face.
"I loved them both dearly," he managed to say between broken
breaths, "Mary showed me the other day that I have to try to honor
them by living a better life."

"Do you mean Mrs. Wilson, I think she knew your wife," I said

"Yes, I sort of remember her, she knew my wife quite well,
but I never knew her back then, just someone my wife knew. She's
right though, my wife would have kept me on the straight and
narrow, and would have wanted me to stay that way. I'd like to try,
but it's kind of a losing fight now."

"It's going to take a lot of will power, I think though that
Robert, George and I would like to help. Mrs. Wilson would help
too I'm sure. Maybe the way to start would be to join the AA.
You could talk about it with others that have been through it,
they also give you a companion to help by calling him during the
real bad times. Why don't we see about that when we get back to
Peterborough."

"How can I say no?"

"I talked to Dave Gransden before we came up. He was telling me his folks played many different instruments. One of his brothers, one of his sisters and his father play in the Salvation Army's brass band in Fenelon Falls at church on Sundays. So I've invited them to come to our BBQ on Saturday. His other siblings also play fiddle and guitars. They have a big family and all play instruments. Dave says they love a good party and would love to come. We should have a great band as John and Will are bringing their instruments.

Saturday all was ready for the barbecue except the steaks, so George and I went to town to pick them up. They were beauties. The sun was shining and the temperature was just right, a beautiful fall day. The crowd started arriving at noon. People came by boat, car and on foot. Mary had even brought her boyfriend Ken. Everyone had heard of the arrests of the gang in Peterborough and of our involvement. Some of it was false and we tried to play down some of the wilder rumors at least. The atmosphere was one of high good humor. Midway through the afternoon I found myself sitting with Dave's girlfriend. He had talked her into coming. Her name was Lesley Nichols, and she lived with her family on a farm between Bobcaygeon and Fenelon Falls.

"I'm glad Dave asked you to come," I said, "are you having a good time?"

"Yes, thank you, I am," she replied.

"Are you still going to school, and if so what grade are you in?"

Yes, I was going to Fenelon High, I just finished grade 13."

"Any plans for higher education?"

"I wanted to be a veterinarian, but we can't afford that, so I'm not sure just now."

"That's a profession that hasn't had a lot of women involved. What made you think of that?"

"I love animals of all sorts, and I know something about them. Everyone on our farm has to pull their weight."

"Our vet was just saying the other day that his practice is getting too big for him. Do you have a summer job?

It's nice of you to think of me, but even so I can't go on. It would probably mean moving to Toronto or somewhere like that and I couldn't afford the room and board, let alone the tuition and books."

"It must be too late to get in this year anyway, but lots of people take a year off."

"Yes it's too late now, but even with a year off, I have to be practical. Things are not likely to change."

"Money is a big obstacle. I don't mean to get your hopes up only to shatter them again, but I think things could work out. Let me ask around."

"That's nice of you, but there is something else."

"Can I be told what it is?"

"I'm not supposed to tell just yet, Dave and I are engaged and going to marry sometime this fall. Please don't say I told you."

"Congratulations, he's a great guy. You can count on me I won't tell. Even so, going on to school is not completely out. Maybe this is even better. Leave it with me. Let me get you something to drink and we'll toast the happy event."

George was in his heaven telling jokes. Mid-afternoon we got the steaks started, there were a few who didn't want one, but we had plenty of hamburgers and hot dogs and most of the children wanted hot dogs. We also had some barbecued fish. It was a kind of slow process as we could only do about ten steaks at a time, but nobody was in a rush, the people who were hungriest got theirs first. In the evening we toasted or in some cases offered up marshmallows as burnt offerings. Many people came to say that the barbecues had made the summer for them and they hoped we could do the same next year. I had plenty of offers of money to help with cost as well as offers for food and drink for next year. George had got extra fireworks. The band was outdoing themselves. We had a real orchestra. The singing and dancing went until everyone was exhausted. The kids loved the fireworks, and all except the very young hung on until the bitter end which was around 1:00 A.M.

Sunday we all went into Bobcaygeon to church, even Ralph. No typos to give us a laugh, but a really good sermon. That was about all we could manage for Sunday, everyone was tired from the night before. We did a little swimming in the afternoon. Listened to the news on the radio, and went early to bed.

Monday we held our council of war. We all felt that although we had made great progress with the jailing of the burglary gang, we had many loose ends to tie up.

"The robbers are saying they didn't kill Sam," said George, "I can't see how it could be anyone else. He had no enemies and I don't see how it could have been Penner even if he had a sort of motive. He just didn't have the opportunity. I'll grant you he's greedy enough."

"For my money, it has to be them," put in Robert, "there is no one else."

"I've been thinking, as Sherlock Holmes says, you eliminate everything that doesn't fit and what's left must be the truth," I said.

"What doesn't fit?" said Robert.

"I mean if they really didn't do it," I replied. "I have an idea, I just don't want to say anything just yet, it's kind of wild and I need to do a little checking before I put it forward. I'll look into it next week. We still have a lot of other things to think about. In particular young Ray Cavanagh. I don't think there is anything

235

we could do, that wouldn't be frowned upon, and all else aside I wouldn't want anyone, including him to start life in jail. I know he's obnoxious but we can hope he rethinks things," I said, "If his brother is convicted and maybe hanged, surely it would give him pause to think at least."

"I agree," said George, "I know he doesn't have much in redeeming qualities that we can see. I do think we need to be very careful though."

"We must try to keep at least two of us together, as much as we can at least. He may watch us to see if he can get us alone, particularly you, Ron," said Robert.

"Things should be better when we're in Peterborough," I replied, "I'm planning on closing the cottage on Thanksgiving week end that should lessen the threat somewhat. That's weeks away yet. We could come up a couple of times in the winter for some hunting, there are some good areas around here for both geese and deer. The problem is it leaves Mary somewhat vulnerable."

"He seems obsessed with us just now," said George, "maybe he'll forget about her for a while."

"We can only hope," I said. "Let's go down to Peterborough Friday. I need to get a car for there, and I want to see if the police are getting anywhere with Jimmy Cavanagh. We can fly down and get you to drive us in from the airport."

John Schell started on the hanger on Tuesday. We had decided to build to our own specifications, making the main room big enough to accommodate a bigger plane than I was buying, and a large well equipped workshop on the back with bench saw, lathes, metal and wood, as well as sanders, joiners and everything conceivable to work on any project we might like to construct or fix. The main front door was to lift to the ceiling, with a separate door into the work shop. I hired Paul, to check on the cottage once in a while at odd hours. We arranged for him to take the walkie talkie we had with us and talked to the police about what he was to do. They said it would be okay to call them in an emergency.

First thing Friday morning we climbed into the 170 and Robert flew us to Peterborough. His car was still in the airport parking lot so we climbed in and he took George home and me to the car dealers. I looked at a few new models and settled on a Studebaker Golden Hawk, I had admired the lines of the Studebaker for a few years. I had to order one to be delivered later next week as they didn't have one in stock with all the bells and whistles. 1956 models were produced with all sorts of things listed as options, even turn signals. We finally settled on color and the other options. The salesman and I talked briefly about having a mobile phone installed. It would take up most of the trunk and I would need to set up a call through an off shore operator, like a walkie talkie. They had kept the basic cost down by making many things as options. The car was expensive with options, but it was what I wanted, and as Robert was always saying, if you've got it, use it. I had earlier given my sons each a large amount of their inheritance, so I might as well have fun. Like Robert said he had so far never seen a hearse with a trailer on the back filled with a person's worldly goods. Finally Robert drove me to a rental car place and I got one for the week.

When I got to my house, Mrs MacGregor had a nice meal of lamb garnished with many vegetables. She didn't think I ate enough vegetables. Saturday we went to the races. John had one of Jake Sheldrake's horses and Dorset Lightning running. He told us he didn't have Sundown Sheila running anymore as he had earlier bred her to Joe Handley's stallion, she'd have her foal early next year. As he had warned they were tired, neither one wound up in the money. Time for a rest. They had provided a lot of fun and some good wins throughout the summer. As I was leaving I ran into Harry White the track manager, and Kurt.

"I haven't seen much of you and your friends this summer," said Harry by way of hello, "I hear you were instrumental in helping to round up that violent bunch of burglars."

"Well I guess we did help a little, but I hear it's being blown out of proportion to what we really did. Still I'm glad to have them finally behind bars," I said.

"Looks like your horses need a rest," said Harry, "they did pretty well all summer though."

"Yes," I replied, "better than we expected, but all good things come to an end. We'll give them some rest, before we bring them back."

"Don't leave them out to pasture too long," he said, "we've got some good races planned for later this fall, I'd like to see them run in some. They were the stars of the track for most of the summer."

I took my leave and thoughtfully headed home.

Church on Sunday, we were delighted to see the secretary was still at it. She had adorned the bulletin with "Potluck supper Sunday at 5:00 PM - prayer and medication to follow." She was a gem. The sermon had been on the prodigal son. The pastor could certainly give a stirring sermon. It was well presented. After church I picked up Ralph and we all returned to my house for a Board game night. Mrs. MacGregor's roast beef dinner, was

superb. John had come in from the farm. We played Parcheesi
and Clue before trying our hand at the scrabble board. Ralph had
managed to get to an AA meeting Saturday. Mrs Wilson told him
she was proud of him. He was all smiles. The rest of the night was
spent around the Monopoly board, the game being played while
watching the Ed Sullivan show. The headliner was Elvis Presley.
I personally didn't see anything to upset me by his performance,
nor did any of the others. Paul called late to say he had made a
sweep past the cottage about 9:30 P.M. and found the boat house on
fire, he had called the fire department and the police, but nothing
could be done to save it. Nothing could be done by us either, but we
would fly up Monday to see the damage.

Monday before flying north to the cottage we went to the arena
and got season tickets for the Pete's, they had been the Kitchener
Canucks last year and had done quite well, giving us high hopes of
an entertaining hockey season.

We got in the plane and Robert flew us to the cottage. The
hanger was taking shape, but we immediately headed for the lake.
The boat house was indeed a pile of ashes. The old launch had been
inside and it too had taken us for its last cruise around the lake.
The runabout was a write off, someone had put an ax through it
in several places. Our canoe had been treated to the same ax. The

motor on the runabout had been on the boat, and apparent the ax had been used on it. I called my insurance man and passed on the bad news. We got in the car and went in to the police. They listened to all we said, and mentioned that they were looking for Ray Cavanagh, to explain his whereabouts on Sunday night. He hadn't been home according to his mother, he had been in Peterborough since Friday night she said. The police told us they had found a five gallon can of gasoline by the cottage. It began to look like Paul had arrived in the nick of time. He said he hadn't seen anyone around, but admitted that he had been concentrating on the boat house. At the very least, our fishing was to be totally interrupted for the fall. After my insurance had looked at things, I would wait until spring to get us new boats. We would have to stick to the trout streams. The diner served us up our pork chop lunch. Paul was at the cottage when we returned.

"What are you going to do," he asked.

"Well, I guess it's another job for our hanger builder," I replied, "once he's done with the hanger of course. They obviously meant to fire the cottage as well, you must have arrived before they had a chance. Do you think a couple of your friends would be interested in a few dollars? I'd like to expand your patrols out this way for a while at least. I think you saved the cottage. I wouldn't like to see whoever did this to come back and finish it."

"I can come out this way much more often, but as you suggest, I can ask a friend or two, if they can do some patrolling in addition to the patrols I do."

"I now have no boats, we'll be using your trout streams for a while. Do you know where we could rent a boat for the Thanksgiving weekend? We'd like to do a little last week end trolling."

"The marina in town has boats to rent. I don't know whether they keep them in the water that late, but you can ask."

The cottage was a depressing place with the boat house in ruins.

John Schell arrived. "I guess we have another job for you," I said. "We'll have to wait in any case until the insurance people have a look, but I guess it'll be a job for next spring."

"I guess you'll want the hanger done first," said John, "we should have it mostly enclosed by the end of next week. Then we can clean up the waterfront if your insurance people okay it."

We got back into the 170 and flew back to Peterborough, in a thoughtful mood. George suggested visiting the police and found they had been questioning Jimmy and his friends very closely. They had found a small whip at the farm house and one of Jimmy's buddies had broken down and confessed to the beating of myself.

He claimed Jimmy had done it and the other accused had rubbed the salt in. Jimmy and henchmen were still maintaining they had nothing to do with Sam's death.

That night Paul called, they had caught Ray Cavanagh and his pals firing the hanger, the police had them. The hanger was gone. One of the young lads had been burned badly, when a can of gasoline exploded on them. I felt a bit sick, but we still had the cottage. I thanked Paul and told him we would be up in the morning. It seemed that young bunch would never learn. Lately it seemed that we were either flying to the cottage or back to Peterborough.

John Schell was upset, one could tell, but he assured me he could do the clean up and get it rebuilt before the snow started for the winter. I had insured it as soon as it was started, but how the insurance would be applied was anyone's guess as it was enclosed but not completed inside. I asked him to go ahead as soon as the insurance company had a look at it. My old car which had been parked near the cottage hadn't escaped totally either, but aside from some dents which could be fixed in a body shop, it was okay. We went into Bobcaygeon. We talked to the police and told them what the Peterborough police had told us. It had been an expensive summer, even after the insurance company paid out for the claims.

Some difficult problems had been solved, but we still didn't know for certain about Sam's murder. I was already depressed about the cottage, but this uncertain situation made it worse. Time to put my vague idea to the test. At the very least it looked as if that was our only line left. Everyone, including the police were satisfied that things were wrapped up. Something kept saying to me that it wasn't true. I had a couple of letters to write, then the answers to wait for. 'We shall see' I thought.

Chapter 18

While waiting for a reply from the letters, we spent the next couple of weeks golfing and joy riding in the 170. Slowly we were getting our flying skills back up to a reasonable level. We flew to Toronto to watch a football game between the Hamilton Tiger Cats and the Toronto Argos. While there we also took in a harness race meet and a day at the flats. We flew to Chapleau to see if we could get out fishing, but since we didn't know anyone around, we flew back home disappointed after a couple of false starts. Chapleau looked like a good fishing spot. The locals said there was a fellow that took people sometimes, he was off the main roads, but if we came on a Sunday, he sometimes went to one of the local Churches. He had to ski out in the winter as the road he was on wasn't plowed so we would have to catch him before the snows started. We did a couple of other small flights in between our golfing.

The letters finally came back. When I read them, I was uncertain of what had happened, however, how to get at the truth was the big question. The letters answered some questions but set up many more. I felt the best plan was to get the gang together and hatch a plan.

In the middle of the week we three drove out to John's place. He was in the middle of exercising a couple of horses. He finished and handed over the reins to Dave, before inviting us in for a coffee. Dave had nothing but praise for the BBQ. His family had enjoyed every minute. His girlfriend was quite impressed also.

John had called to tell us he had two horses from our request for some horse to race each other. We went to the farm to look them over.

"This one looks a lot like Kingston Kenny," said George.

"He certainly does," said John. "Except he's a gelding, otherwise there is a couple of other differences. He is nowhere near as good a runner. He's just not as fast as Kingston Kenny but should be able to win some lower class races."

"I think I'd like that one anyway," said George. I knew George had difficulty, even telling if a horse was gelded and half the time he was unsure of whether a horse was a mare or a stallion.

The other horse was a good looking Bay mare that John assured us was about the same class as the Kingston Kenny look alike.

"I like the look of the mare," said Robert. "Can you get the papers made out to show George and myself as the owners? We can get the money for them to you for tomorrow, if that's satisfactory."

"We still need one for me," I said. "I don't care about the color or configuration as you know, just that they need to be in the same approximate class."

"I guess you would want me to train them for you. If we did that, the three horses would have to race as one entry in any race. That's to prevent cheating within the barn." said John. Yes no problem with the papers, they are in my name at present."

"We have no intentions of cheating," said George, "we just thought it might be fun racing against each other. What do you mean when you say they'll have to race as an entry?"

"If more than one horse has the same owner or trainer then they have to be bet on as if they are one unit. They would have to be 1A, 1B and 1C so if you bet on one horse you get all three. If one of them wins, the bet on number one wins, no matter which is the actual winner.

"It could be done, but it might upset some of these folks, particularly those people who love to bet. The betting odds would be very low on an entry. Let me think about it." said John. "No problem finding horses, there's always plenty around. For the present we'll train them a little here and see if they're ready to run. If they are we can have them in a race in about two weeks."

We returned to town in a good frame of mind. Now to try and get some proof of my thoughts on Sam's murderer. After Sunday dinner at my place, I opened the subject. There was only George and Robert there.

"I think I know now who the murderer is, but how to get proof," I said.

"Who is it," asked George.

"I'd rather not say who I think it is just now, just listen and all will be revealed. We need to kind of sneak up I think. We need to set up a trap at the race track. That's where I think it happened."

"Why the track," asked Robert, clearly puzzled. "He was at his house in bed."

"I think he was snatched from the track and taken to his place and killed later that night, to confuse things. That's why I think we've been barking up the wrong tree."

"He would have had to be kidnapped in the middle of the day and held until later," said George. "The autopsy said he had been killed around 10 P.M."

"That was just smoke screen to throw all of us off, police included. It worked to perfection. That's the reason why we need to sneak up on this."

"Well what do you think we should do?" asked George. "You know we'll be happy to help, particularly if we get our man."

"Do you think we could get one of the OPP to come along in case it turns rough?" I said. "You are the buddy of the police force George, could you ask them? We should be in their good books just now."

"I'll ask, but they are going to ask for details."

"Quite likely, just explain as I did to you, hopefully they'll send someone, but we can manage without. I would like to see us do this next Thursday, there will not be any racing so we should have the track to ourselves. I'll talk to Harry at the track and arrange everything else, all I ask is for you two to be there to help."

"I'll certainly be there. You can count on me, even though it sounds kind of dangerous. Are you sure we can handle it ourselves?" said George.

"Nothing is certain. That's why we need to get help if we can from the police, no way of telling what will happen, but I hope it doesn't get violent.

"I wouldn't miss it," said Robert.

Next morning, I went to the track and talked to Harry, telling him I had a special project on and wanted his help and his two security men. I asked him to meet with us next Thursday afternoon at one o'clock to discuss arrangements. He was mystified when I wouldn't tell him more about it, but promised his help. Next I visited Moishe and talked him into taking next Thursday afternoon off.

George called later to say that the OPP had indeed promised an officer for Thursday.

Ray Cavanagh and his friends were brought before the courts on charges of burning my boathouse and hanger. It appeared like the one who had been burned, would eventually recover, but would be scarred badly. It was only to be a preliminary hearing but we were asked to attend. The judge denied them bail and held them over for trial. They just sat there glowering in our direction, as if to say 'you caused this to happen to us'. Some people never learn.

Thursday arrived and all parties gathered at the track at about 12:45 P.M. Harry called for his two security people to join us. I had particularly asked Moishe to look closely at everyone. When the security guys joined us he went white as a sheet and yelled "My God it's Guenther," He immediately started to pass out. Harry who was nearest grabbed him. Kurt took one look and started running to the door to escape. He pulled his gun as he ran. George and the OPP officer bumped into each other in their haste to apprehend him. He hit George hard in the head and that knocked George into the officer. Kurt got through the door, we ran toward the door. As we got through it we saw that Kurt had drawn his gun and while running he was turned to shoot at us. We started to scramble out of the way. Ralph Davidge was there, having seen us go into the office he had walked over to have a short talk to us. He threw an empty garbage can which was lying nearby at Kurt. It hit him just below the knees. He fell hard. Ralph jumped on him and tried to hold him, he took quite a beating until the OPP officer and the rest of us arrived to subdue Kurt. He struggled hard. Ralph got his head bashed against the ground and his face ground into the pavement. The OPP man finally got the cuffs on Kurt who continued to struggle, so we sat on him while the officer called for backup.

When Kurt had been driven away, we went back inside. Moishe had recovered a little from his faint and was able to explain that the man we knew as Kurt was really an ex-guard from their prison camp during the war. Moishe felt he was the cruelest of the guards at Bergen-Belsen where he and Sam had been for most of the war. His name was Guenther Schembekler. How he had wound up in security in Peterborough we had no way of knowing.

The news hounds began to arrive. I had to explain to everyone that my distrust of Nazis was at the bottom of my reasoning to think of him. I liked most German people, but in my opinion Nazis were crazy. I had written to the Defense office to ask about Kurt Mueller who had been in a prisoner of war camp near Oshawa until war's end. Their return letter said that Kurt Mueller had been

251

found murdered in Oshawa a month after release. All I could think of was if this guy was not Kurt Mueller then who was he and what was he doing here. Ralph had been taken to hospital to get his cuts and bruises looked after. The media people were talking about him as a hero. That was fine by us, if he hadn't taken a hand in things Kurt/Guenther might easily have escaped. When all questions were exhausted we went to the hospital to see how Ralph was doing.

"I never liked that guy," said Ralph when we met him in the outpatients after he had received treatment. "He always made fun of me because of my drinking. What was he running from?"

"We think he's the guy that murdered Sam," said George, ever cautious. "Nothing has yet been proved, we don't even know how he did it."

"He must have recognized Sam," said Moishe, "and realized the game was up."

"He kept Sam alive until later in the evening, then made it look like the burglars were at fault," I said, "that's my theory anyway. We have to go over to the police station now to make our statements. I guess we'll find out sooner or later the whole story. Do you want to come with us Ralph they'll want your statement as well."

"Yes," said Ralph "I'm looking forward to it."

The OPP had got the gist of it from Moishe before leaving for the station. They took our statements and let us go home. They would take things from here. Instead we took Moishe to the Italian restaurant for a nice pasta supper, he was still shaken. We would have to wait for an explanation as to what had happened.

Sunday's sermon was on 'the wages of sin'. As the pastor later said, we had a lot of sinners pushing us hard from all sides all summer. Thank heavens it seemed to be over finally. The sermon was well prepared and well received. Our friends had to hear all the details. We had talked Ralph into coming to the service. He was hailed as a conquering hero. He loved it. The secretary had missed her chance for a funny in the bulletin. That was a nice change.

George was able to find out through the police fraternity that Guenther had struck a kind of bargain, if he pleaded guilty he would get off without being executed, but get a life sentence only. He pleaded guilty to Sam's murder as well as the murder of the real Kurt Mueller. It turned out that he and Kurt had both come from the same small town in Germany and had known each other. Guenther had learned from his relatives during the war where Kurt was being held in the prisoner of war camp near Oshawa. He escaped Germany near the end of the war, just a few steps ahead of the Military Police, by boarding a tramp steamer out of the Netherlands and jumping ship in Halifax. He had then gone to Oshawa looked up Kurt, found out Kurt had applied for a job at the track in Peterborough without being known personally to Harry. He had then killed Kurt and took his identification and proceeded to Peterborough.

We spent most of this time on the golf course and driving range interspersed with joy riding around Ontario in the 170. The new plane was expected to arrive shortly after Thanksgiving. The Tuesday night prior to Thanksgiving John happened to be up early to look in on one of his charges that had a slight case of colic. A shot rang out and a horse in one of the fields started screaming. John ran outside just as another shot was fired. The horse was in a paddock close to the barn. A car suddenly started and sped away from the other side of the paddock, John got a good look at it before it totally disappeared. A horse was down in pain. John ran in and called the vet and the police. The horse was the one George had bought. It had to be put down it was shot in both front legs. John went into the house and got a gun. He walked out and shot the horse in the head. He hated to see animals suffer. The police arrived and began asking questions. John told them all he knew. They asked why the horse was shot. John could only speculate but said it might have something to do with its appearance. He told them about the troubles with McKenzie's stables and how they were a violent bunch. Maybe they had thought the horse to be Kingston Kenny as the two looked much alike particularly from a distance. Two spent cartridges were found near were John had seen the car. The police had already been headed for the Mackenzie farm, when they arrived they had a search warrant and proceeded to search finding and confiscating a possible gun.

We badly need some rest so we went early to the cottage, taking Ralph along. We had no trouble renting a boat, and were fishing the same evening. It was good to be able to relax finally after a hectic summer. Ralph seemed to be well on the way to kicking the alcohol on a permanent basis. As he said it would be a long struggle yet, but he'd made a good start.

Sitting talking that night, George felt it was time to loosen up with a joke.

"In honor of our burglars I have a good one for you, that also shows that crime doesn't pay," said George.

"This burglar who always worked alone had a habit of casing out a house that looked prosperous. He would wait until the occupants appeared to be away for the night and then go to work. He finds such a house and when all seems clear he sneaks over to it, breaks the glass in the door window, and proceeds into the house. As he's sneaking down the hallway, he hears a voice say

'Jesus is watching you!' He is alert immediately, but when nothing else happens, he decides he must be hearing things, so he keeps going. Again he hears a voice say 'Jesus is watching you!' So he turns on his flashlight, and he sees this parrot in a cage. He says to the parrot 'Did you speak?' The parrot says 'Yes I did.' 'What's your name?' says the burglar. 'My name is Clyde.' Says the parrot. The burglar asks 'Who would name a parrot Clyde?' The parrot replies' The same guy that named the Rottweiler Jesus'

Excerpt from Wages of War

Sequel to Ghost from the Holocaust

Chapter 1

Summer 1947

Suddenly all our planning became a reality. Joe drove the old stake truck in front of the stopped armored car blocking its way forward. The set up cue was when Sarg had shot the guard who had just emerged from the rear door of that armoured car. Sarg was our best shot that's why he had been selected for that job. He was a block away on King Street. He was to have used a rifle with a telescopic sight. As planned I now pulled the stolen car I was driving in behind and reversed with the trunk to the rear of the armoured car so they couldn't reverse. The shot guard did us a favour and fell blocking the door open. Dave who was in a suit standing on the curb was to have grabbed the door. Instead he pulled his pistol, stepped to the door and shot the other guard inside the rear compartment. Joe jumped from the old stake truck onto the armoured car and setup the interference to block communication. Then he covered both doors so that the driver and guard inside the front didn't try to be heroes. I yanked open both back doors of the car I was driving and opened the trunk, to receive the money bags. Dave and I then entered the rear compartment of the armoured car. The guard inside was only wounded not dead. Dave disarmed

him and gave him a kick in the ribs to discourage heroics. Then we

started grabbing as many money bags as we could. We put them in

my car and went for more as fast as we were able. Sarg had arrived

with the other car by that time and had the trunk open to accept

more bags, if there were any. He had to leave the back seat open for

Joe. The guard from the bank, where the money had been destined,

beside which all this action was taking place joined the fray at

that point and started shooting at us. He hit Sarg. Sarg went down

heavy and looked to be dead. We had seen a lot of dead people.

Joe shot at the bank guard and scored a hit. The hit didn't look

serious as the bank guard dove back into the bank. Joe jumped

from the stake truck ran to us and jumped into the car Sarg had

brought. Dave and I hopped in our car and we both sped away. We

got several blocks away before we heard any sirens. We just slowed

down like good law abiding citizens.

Dave and I headed for the small warehouse we used. Joe got

there just ahead of us. We had left the door open so we both drove

straight in. Joe jumped out and closed the door to the warehouse.

"We should be okay in here," said Joe. "It's a pretty rundown neighbourhood. Nobody lives nearby. There was nobody on the street to see us arrive."

"Let's hope that is the case," said Dave.

"We better get the loot into our car and get out of here as soon as possible," I said. "We can leave Sarg's in here with this car we stole last night."

"We should take Sarg's car with us, he might be mad at us if we don't," said Dave.

"Nah leave it," said Joe, "Richie's right, Sarg is dead, we all saw him. We've seen plenty of dead guys when we were overseas during the war. Somebody may have spotted it and got the license plate number. Let's just pick up Randy and head north like we planned."

"I may be right, but maybe not," I replied, "too bad Randy had to work today, but we had to keep the deception going until the last. We were lucky to get him inside the armour car company, so that we had all that inside information. We can't leave him behind now."

"Where is he meeting us?" asked Dave.

"At the west end of the Bloor streetcar line in about an hour," I said. "Just enough time for us to get the money into our getaway car. Let's get a move on here."

Sarg, Randy and I had been in the original squad on "D" Day. Other guys had been added to the squad at later times throughout the war. Only four others of our squad had survived through to the completion of what was now called the Second World War. One had gone back to his wife on the family potato farm near Victoria Harbour in Prince Edward Island. Dave and Joe were here with us and Peter was our get-away hideout in Lindsay.

We were proud members of the King's Rifles when we charged ashore in the middle of Juno beach on D day. We were cut to pieces as a unit. The guy beside me when we hit the water had been shot while we were still in the water. The wound had looked fatal but I had tried to grab him. All I got was his dog tags as his body was swept out to sea. I had stuck them in my pocket and thought nothing of them for a few days. That's when I got the 'Dear John' letter from my girl back home. She was married to my worst enemy. He was the town bully as we were growing up. So I had taken the guy's dog tags and become him. We had reported me missing in action to get back at her. Sarg and Randy were the only ones who knew my true identity and now Sarg was gone.

If we had been able to find jobs, maybe we wouldn't have got talked into this robbery foolishness. Now Sarg was dead. He had kept most of us going during the war. Now we couldn't help him anymore. The money we had, however much it was didn't seem worth it somehow. The six of us were at loose ends. Randy and Dave were from Toronto originally. Joe was from Newmarket. Dave's parents were still living and so were Joe's, but neither had any other attachments. Randy's parents had died before he went overseas. Randy had contributed most to this robbery. He got a job at the Armour car company, and had found out the times and the vehicle to be used for the big payroll deliver to the downtown banks. He had even managed to get a duplicate key made for the rear money compartment. We hadn't needed it though as it had turned out.

"We've got lots of time," I said. "I don't think we should hang around here though. Who knows what people have seen and will report to the authorities? We'll go have lunch at that diner just north of High Park on Bloor."

"What time does Randy get off work?" asked Dave.

"He gets off at noon," I said. "We'll meet him shortly after that."

"We should get him something to eat, maybe a couple of sandwiches to go, he'll probably be hungry."

"Good idea. We'll get out of the city, but it's going to be way too early to go to Lindsay. We need to get there after dark so we don't make a big show of getting to Peter's house. The less people know or see the better."

"What are we going to do in the mean time?" asked Joe.

"We'll drive around a bit, maybe have dinner in Barrie. That's a big enough place that people shouldn't take too much notice of us and it's sort of in the wrong direction. Then even if we might be identified somehow, it would still be misleading. We'll try to get to Lindsay about 9 P.M."

Chapter 2

10 Years Later
Spring 1957

It was a beautiful Saturday afternoon. The kind of spring day that gave a person the feeling that summer would be sensational. We were in our favorite place, the harness horse racetrack at Peterborough. Since George and Robert had each gotten a separate trainer, we were able to race against each other without being an entry. We were all entered in the third race, a low level claimer. At the moment harness horse racing was our favorite sport. During the winter we had been cheering for the Peterborough Petes. Their arena had not been ready for them to play at the start of the hockey year, maybe that was why they hadn't done well in their first season.

The horses were all called to the starting gate. George, Robert and I were excited to see how our horses would do against each other. This was the first race of the season for all three. We all had our hopes up. I had retained John as my trainer, he was also an old family friend. Will his hired hand would be my driver as usual.

This was a new horse for me. John had bought me the horse over the winter. Its name was Ocean Ann, a roan mare. She had good breeding, just not blessed with great speed.

Robert's horse was a bay mare. She had similar speed to both my horse and George's dark brown gelding which was called Armstrong Sunlight. Robert's horse had the name of Blythe Spirit. The trainers of Robert and George's horses were both small time trainer's. They didn't have an in house driver so they were both employing catch drivers for today's race.

The starting gate was moving, all six pacers moving well. The gate swung wide and pulled away. The race was on. George's gelding Armstrong Sunlight dropped into second at the rail, behind the early leader. Robert's Blythe Spirit was running fourth also at the rail. Will had my Ocean Ann back in fifth, only ahead of one other horse. Going down the backstretch for the first time Blythe Spirit pulled out and started to edge up on the third place horse. 'Too early' I thought. It did however allow Will to gain a little ground with my Ocean Ann without going outside of the windbreak created by the leaders. They came by the grandstand the first time in that order. Blythe Spirit had lost a little ground on the third place horse on the turn, but was still coming on slowly.

Around the next corner nothing was changed until that corner was finished, then as they turned into the back stretch, the driver on George's Armstrong Sunlight, pulled out to challenge the horse that had been leading up until now. Before the club house turn Will pulled out with Ocean Ann, and moved past Blythe Spirit in a rush so he was not three wide on the last turn. At the wire the horse that had been leading all the way hung on gamely to win by a neck over George's horse. Will had been able to get my horse up for third by a head. None of our horses had won, but it was still a decent outing.

We all rushed down to the finish as our horses were being led out. It had been an exciting race. John came to see if Ocean Ann had come through the race in good shape. Will assured him that she had, and when John had looked her over, Will led her back to the barn.

John said, "I just have Jake Sheldrake's Sim's Delight going this afternoon. He's in a good spot to win and Jake has just bought a new horse for me to train."

"With my two going to the main circuit in Toronto to run that will leave you with a few stalls open anyway," I said. "How are the new mothers to be coming along?"

"Mothers are doing well."

"Yes well my mare was a good looking mare, just couldn't run very fast. How about your horse Sundown Sheila?"

"She too is doing well. We've got a nice start going for my stud farm. Dave and Lesley are excited about going to Toronto with Dorset Lightning and Kingston Kenny on Monday."

"It's great to be able to send my two best horses, I hope they do well in the big city. Dave has turned into a good race horse trainer and Lesley a good help after her brief stint with your vet. She says she's learned a lot. I hope she gets into vet school later this fall."

"They are both very enthusiastic about this chance."

Church on Sunday the secretary had kept up her tradition. She had written 'don't let worry kill you off - let the Church help.' Our secretary never seemed to see the humor in what she wrote. The sermon itself was great. Pastor Alton had started a new series based on Solomon's wisdom. After church we all gathered at my house for one of Mrs. MacGregor's roast beef dinners. Ralph Davidge was there with his new wife Mary. She was quite proud of him as he had kept off the alcohol for more than six months now. He had even set up a small landscaping business, just cutting grass and doing the weeding for his customers. It was going well.

George was in fine form. Telling a new joke, I sometimes thought he told jokes to forget about all the things he had seen as a policeman before he had retired. Robert had been Royal Air Force fighter command. He didn't like to remember those days as his loved ones had all been killed in Nazi raids over London. Moishe our friend who had survived Bergen-Belsen concentration camp and Jim our banker friend rounded out my company today. I liked having my friends to dinner. My name is Ron Withers born into an affluent family. I had only my two sons and their families. All my parents and my beloved wife had passed away as well.

It was a great way to finish a Sunday. We all ate too much. We played a few games and watched the Ed Sullivan show. By that time we were all tired, so we wrapped things up and went our separate ways to get ready for another work week. Most of us were retired but we still called it a work week.

Monday we gathered at the diner for coffee. We planned to go to Toronto. My horses were being shipped there today and Dave and Lesley were moving into my rooming house. We would go and help them unpack. Now that Dave had bought the old pick-up truck, he had enough room to take their belongings without our help. Toronto was just where the action would be today. We would just have to pass up our golf game for this Monday. Dave and Lesley would be moving into the apartment that Dave had occupied last summer. The furniture and everything was still as he'd left it. I hadn't been able to rent it since. We intended to head for Toronto after we had finished our coffee.

"What was the reason you sent Dorset Lightning to Toronto this time?" asked Robert.

"Well he's looking even better this year and he did win some good races at Morrow Park last year'" I replied. "It also gives Dave two horses to look after and I think Dorset Lightning should be given his chance at this higher competition level."

"There's a lot more to this racing thing than I thought at first. I never realised. Since I now have my own horse to yell at I've been much more interested," said Robert.

"That's exactly how I feel about it," said George. "Previously I was just looking at it from a policeman's point of view. Lots of opportunities for criminal activities."

"That's for certain," I replied, "but if everyone plays it straight, it can be a lot of fun. The trouble always is that people are greedy and will go to almost any lengths to win money. The other thing is that very few ever run too far against the law. It's very seldom that someone gets into real trouble for their track criminal activities."

With our coffee finished we headed for Toronto and the rooming house I owned on Galley Avenue near High Park. With me driving we got there before Dave and Lesley. My main tenant came out to meet us.

"Glad to see you again," he said. "Thanks for the letter letting me know that the nice young fellow who was here last year is coming back. I like him."

"Thanks for helping him out last year when he was being beat up," I said. "I sincerely hope that nonsense has been taken care of, we're looking forward to a quiet year."

"You were saying he's now married and will have his new wife with him. I look forward to meeting her."

"You'll like her as well. She's a really nice person. They should be along anytime now. We came to see them settled in."

We went in and up to the second floor which was to be Dave's apartment. "Very sparsely furnished," I said.

"They're not used to a lot," said Robert. "I don't think they're expecting to be given things on a silver platter."

"You're right as always," I replied "but I think I'd like to give them a 'moving in' present. They wouldn't say anything, but that old cot really isn't suitable as a marriage bed. You and George stay here and help them get established. I'll see what can be done. I'll be back shortly."

I'd seen a furniture story nearby on Dundas Street when we were coming into the city. I went there and found a nice King size bed that was at a good price. I bought it including box spring and mattress and arranged for it to be delivered the next day. When I got back to the house, Dave and Lesley had arrived. George and

Robert had helped them move into the apartment. They were quite excited. It was the first time in a big city for Lesley. I explained were I had been.

"We can't take that," said Dave. "You've already been too good to us. We never in our lives expected a great opportunity like this to start with. To work and learn here in the city is enough."

"I can't cancel it now" I said. "I have a special job for you, if you feel this gift is too much, this could be as payment for looking after this for me. I want you Lesley to watch as many 2 and 3 year old stakes races as you can manage and look for a good 1 or 2 horses who would make a good stud to stand at John's or for a good brood mare. Besides I want you well rested so you can get up early and exercise the horse and get them ready for their races. Let's finish up here and all of us go down to the track and see if the horses have arrived?"

"Well, okay if you put it that way, but I would tackle this job for you without that as incentive"

"However you want to do this for me. I want to get a couple of good horses to help John establish his stud farm. I don't know much about that part of racing but I think a share in a stud is calculated on how many mares the stud can cover in a season. I want to give you and John a share each, so that you can breed your own race horse or sell your share."

"Let's find this horse first. I'll do my best for you. With incentive like that, I'll be looking hard."

Dave and Lesley went to the local grocery store and got a few things to get them going on the week's food.

We got into our cars and proceeded to the track and around to the barn where Dorset Lightning and Kingston Kenny were to be kept. They had arrived and John's friend, who was our Toronto trainer and Will who had brought the horses from Peterborough were busy getting them settled with food and water. Bert Mackie who was John's Toronto trainer had already entered Dorset Lightning in a claiming race on Thursday. So we decided to stay until Thursday and see him run. We chatted for a while. The clouds had closed in and a steady rain had started. It looked like it was going to keep raining all day. George knew of an 'all you can eat' buffet restaurant in the east end, so we decided to treat Dave and Lesley to dinner. The restaurant was huge, but even being that size the place was crowded. Obviously quite popular. Dave and Lesley had never been to such a place before and were amazed. We had a great meal then went for a walk downtown Toronto. Lots of people out for the night, all of the movie theaters along Yonge Street were doing a lot of business from the 'B' movies up to the large ornate theaters with the first run blockbusters of movies. After a while we stopped our sightseeing walk and retired to a small restaurant for a late coffee before retiring to our hotel. We were soaked but had enjoyed the crowds of people and the glitter of downtown.

It rained almost continually for Tuesday and Wednesday. We saw two good movies The King and I, and the Ten Commandments. Both of these had been nominated for the best picture Oscar of 1956 but had lost out to Around the World in Eighty Days.

Thursday at track time the rain had stopped but it was still overcast. The track was rated sloppy. Dorset Lightning had never run in sloppy conditions, but Dave and Bert felt he might do alright so he was left in although two others were scratched and would not run because of the conditions. Bert's main driver was to have the drive. He took Dorset Lightning to the front as soon as the gate swung open. He had told us he would do that so the horse wouldn't be getting mud splashed in his face early. He held that spot from start to finish. Dorset Lightning had won the biggest purse of his career. He seemed to like the squishy surface to run on. We were glad we had stayed over. Friday morning we headed home to Peterborough.

The rain had lasted until Friday morning. We were able to get back for post time Friday. Our three horses were again entered against each other in the third race. A low level claimer. The track was sloppy just as it had been the day before in Toronto. The driver on Blythe Spirit started her off in fourth place but kept her out of the worst of the mud by staying wide of the other runners. On moving down the back side he took her a bit wider and urged her on to a greater effort. She seemed to be one paced and couldn't respond too well to the urging, but she came on gamely and wound up winning to everyone's surprise. Robert was very excited and insisted we had to go to the bar with him and have a liqueur. Robert opted for a scotch whiskey while George and I had a small Drambuie. None of us drank but to help our friend Robert celebrate his first big win we easily made the exception. A great day, a good feeling. We had sown our wild oats today, we would have to go to church on Sunday and pray for crop failure. As George said though, even Jesus drank beer, wine and spirits, we should just 'not pursue strong drink.'

Saturday we went out to John's farm. He had just finished breakfast. We only had Kingston Kenny running that day and he was in Toronto.

"I gave Dave an extra task," I said, "he's to find a good stallion out of the two and three year old stakes horses so I can buy him. Would you be interested in having him stand at stud here at your farm?"

"I'd be very interested and flattered to have him here, but that poses several questions and a few problems," he replied. "When were you planning this purchase?"

"Probably late fall, as we'll all have to have a look at him ourselves before doing anything about the acquisition."

"That helps a lot. The big thing is I don't have the facilities to have a stud standing here at present. I will need a lot more stalls, usually the brood mares are brought here when they are still pregnant from last year's mating. They have their foals here so that they will be ready to mate right after foaling."

"You mean to tell me they get mated right away?" said George.

"Usually the first or second time they come into heat," said John. "The gestation period is 340 days, so they need to get pregnant almost immediately to take advantage of as many years as possible. There is a very narrow window for foals to be born. They become 1 year old January first no matter when they are born. That means they become 2 and are eligible to race in January the next year. How good do you think a 13 month old horse would do against one that may be 23 months old? You have to be careful that doesn't happen."

"On a more practical note for now," I said. "I understand how this is going to cost you money to get to the point of doing all this. How can I best compensate you for this?"

"As far as the barns and stalls are concerned, I think I still have enough money from the last bank loan to build enough stalls to get started. The problem is going to be how to fill them. It depends a lot on the horse you buy for your stud. Most of the time you pay a lot for a real good two or three year old, put him out to stud and find out 3 or 4 years down the road that he can't pass his speed along to his offspring. Now all you have is a six or seven year old horse that has to be returned to the race track to race, and you have to hope he'll win some money toward the expense of buying him in the first place. Most of the time you lose money, lots of it. However you must also understand that this can be one of the greatest investments in the world"

"How do you mean? I wasn't trying to earn money, just get a few well-bred foals to race in the future. We know that John Simpson drove Noble Adios to the win at the Little Brown Jug last fall in a time of two minutes and four fifths of a second, he nearly broke the two minute mile, but I won't be trying to buy Noble Adios for a stud so you can relax a bit, I'm not going to spend that much money."

"Each horse is different of course, so I can't be very precise just at the moment, but if the horse is vigorous he can sometime cover more than a mare a day in the proper season. The better the horse has been on the track and they usually cost the most, then the better chance you have of attracting the top producing mares to come to him. That increases the chances of having foals that can win. Also sometime your stud can only service one mare every few days. If he covers a lot of mares and their offspring win races once they get that older, particularly big stakes races, then the amount you can charge for a placement or a cover, sometimes called a share, goes up to heights you can hardly believe. No matter what you pay for the horse, he can maybe earn that much in a year. That leaves you with many years to earn baskets of money."

"There is a theoretical number which I don't know but early prices for covering a mare is set by dividing that number into the cost price. For instance if the horse cost $10,000 and he can cover 40 mares then the price would be set at $250.00. If his offspring start winning big money that could go up to $2500.00 for a place or cover for instance. Then he would be making $100,000 a year for the owner."

"Wow I didn't realise the money involved."

"The money and costs are many, but if you wanted to pay me in kind for having him stand at stud here at my place, I would accept it that way."

"I understand that there is the feeding and vet cost as well as other things that have to be taken into account, by payment in kind, do you mean you would accept covers to your mares or shares if you like as payment for keeping him here and the costs involved?"

"Yes that's exactly what I mean. I could then sell the 'shares' or covers if I wished or I could get mares to fill the place."

"How about 5 places then?"

"Too generous as always but I accept."

"Let me see if I completely understand what you are saying. Let's say I buy the top horse of the year. A horse that's won all of his two and three year old stakes races. He's never been beaten, in other words. He would cost a huge amount, but he would attract a lot of the best broodmares. The broodmares that have already had foals who have made it to the races and have won races. This horse would then have the best chance of becoming a top notch stud, or he might not be able to pass along his speed to his offspring, and he would be worthless, losing a lot of money for his owner. He could also be able to pass his speed along to the next generation and make huge amounts of money for his owner. This process wouldn't be known for at least two years when the firsts of his offspring start to race. Have I got the facts correct?"

"Yes!"

"Well don't build those barns just yet. I have to think about this for a while. I will say at this time that this idea was not how I was thinking about a stud. You've given me a lot to think about. We'll talk about it again, probably many times"

We chatted for a while longer then Robert, George and I hustled off to get to the golf course for our tee time. We didn't have time for a good practice so our scores were all in the high nineties. We just didn't take it serious enough. We liked the walk but practice was too much like work. While walking back to the clubhouse George said. "We shouldn't be too hard on ourselves like Babe Ruth once said, 'It took me seventeen years to get 3,000 hits in baseball. I did it in one afternoon on the golf course'

We could always count on George to lighten up the situation.

Mrs. McGregor always went to early mass so that she could get to my place in time to cook us an excellent Sunday dinner. Sunday

Pastor Alton preached a good sermon on Ecclesiastes chapter 3 'A Time for Everything'. The secretary had missed an opportunity to make one of her usual mistakes in the bulletin today. No funny comment to liven our afternoon. Mrs. McGregor's dinner and the games evening, were a great success. We enjoyed each other's company.

Printed in the United States
By Bookmasters